The Easter Prayer

An Amish Easter Story

J. Willis Sanders

ISBN: 978-1-954763-59-3 (paperback)
ISBN: 978-1-954763-58-6 (ebook)

BUGGS ISLAND BOOKS

Printed in the United States of America
Cover art by bookcoverzone.com

By J. Willis Sanders
Read more about these books at
https://jwillissanders.wixsite.com/writer

The Eliza Gray Series
The Colors of Eliza Gray
The Colors of Denver Andrews
The Colors of Tess Gray

The Forgiveness Quilt: An Amish Christmas Carol
The Easter Prayer: An Amish Easter Story

The Clara Engelman Series
Clara's Mourning
Coming soon:
Clara's Courtship
Clara's Choice

The Essence of Emmaline Strong

The Outer Banks of North Carolina Series
The Diary of Carlo Cipriani
If the Sunrise Forgets Tomorrow
Love, Jake

The Hope Series
The Coincidence of Hope
The Yearning of Hope
The Gift of Hope

Writing as J. D. James
Reid Stone: Hard as Stone
Reid Stone: Red Rage

Reviews for The Colors of Eliza Gray
https://www.amazon.com/dp/B092RKPZBM

"Captivating! … J. Willis Sanders has captured love in this story. Love of a father to his daughter, love between brothers and sisters, and true love struggling to find a way to a future together. I look forward to Sanders' next book."

"I can honestly say that "The Colors of Eliza Gray" had me hooked from chapter one! It had me wishing for a "happily ever after" for Eliza from the beginning. Every emotion is found in this book and J. Willis Sanders definitely knows how to draw his readers in! I had read half of it before I realized it and finished it up the next morning!"

"Enjoyed this book so much! Stayed up way past my bedtime to finish it. Romantic and inspiring story. Great descriptions enabling the reader to visualize the scenes. Highly recommended."

"You won't be able to put this awesome book down! Love, love of a father and their love!!!! Please write another about how their lives are going!!!"

"The Colors of Eliza Gray is one of the most compelling books I've ever read. Beginning with a hearing-impaired abused Eliza. Taking you through her education and life altering experiences once she has her world opened to her. I truly hated it to end. Can't wait for the next book."

Reviews for The Christmas Quilt: An Amish Christmas Carol
https://www.amazon.com/gp/product/B0BNVQDKD1

"The Forgiveness Quilt is a wonderful book that can be read in one sitting or chapter by chapter. I took it with me on a long journey, and it made the trip so much more enjoyable. The book is well written and engaging throughout, with great descriptions of the setting as well as the characters. I highly recommend this as a pre-Christmas read!"

"This is the first book I have read by J. Willis Sanders but will not be the last. A very uplifting and inspiring book."

"In The Forgiveness Quilt, Sanders set a substantial challenge for himself: to recreate Charles Dickens' journey of writing A Christmas Carol in just six weeks. As a writer myself, I understand how challenging it can be to write just the first draft of story of this length in six weeks, let alone completing all the work necessary for refining the draft and preparing it for publication. With compelling characters, the sad journey of a heart hardening over time, immune to messages of love and joy, and its final, almost too late redemption, Sanders has succeeded in his challenge and created a moving holiday story of hope and redemption."

Reviews for Clara's Mourning: Book One of the Clara Engelman Series
https://www.amazon.com/Claras-Mourning-Book-Clara-Engelman-ebook/dp/B0BW51TCRS

"I just finished Clara's Mourning and it is wonderful! I was drawn to Clara because she recently lost her husband just like me. She now has to learn how to navigate life on their farm without him and raise their two small children alone."

"I have enjoyed every one of this authors books and let me tell you this one is exceptional! Not only do you get a look into another branch of the Amish/ Mennonite culture (Beachy Amish Mennonite) but you get a wonderful story with great characters as well."

"This story captures your attention in the very first chapter and holds it until the very last page! Once you start reading, you just can't put it down and stop reading! Once you finish the book, you can't wait for the next book in this trilogy. The author has a wonderful and descriptive writing style. His characters are very realistic. As a reader, you feel the emotions they are having as you read!"

"A very good book, easy to read. Had great and loveable characters. I loved the story. Keeps you guessing."

Reviews for The Outer Banks of North Carolina Series
https://www.amazon.com/gp/product/B098P67LJB

The Diary of Carlo Cipriani

"This is fascinating tale of survival, both of shipwrecked sailors and of how wild horses came to live on the Outer Banks. I enjoyed the characters and the character development, as well."

"The heartfelt descriptions of the characters brings them to life and bids you to follow their stories. There is life and love, despair and grief that eventually give way to hope for the future. A well written, intriguing story that bids me to learn more about the Outer Banks."

"Many twists and turns, lots of tragedy but always hope. At several points you are not sure what is real and what is the narrators madness due to his loneliness. A very satisfying resolution answers all our questions."

If the Sunrise Forgets Tomorrow

"What a captivating book. I read it in 2 sittings because we just couldn't put it down. Brought tears to my eyes!"

"This book was captivating and it was difficult for me to put it down. If you like a touch of history and have a love for Ocracoke, this is a great book to read. It was very descriptive and made me feel like I was there. Virginia and Ruby are typical sisters who are loving each other one minute and the next they are disagreeing. I enjoyed the strength they displayed as they overcame many obstacles. A Great Read!"

"To be honest, I wasn't certain I would enjoy this book. I've read other books at in the Outer Banks and a lot of them seem to be sloppily written and just capitalizing on the setting to prey on die-hard OBX readers. I was pleasantly surprised to find it very well written and descriptive. It was easy to visualize the island, the characters, and the story as it all unfolded. I would recommend checking it out!"

Reviews for The Coincidence of Hope
https://www.amazon.com/gp/product/B0B2KZ9KPM

"This is not war story, nor an action novel. It's not a love story. No, it's more than that, as it touches on many love stories, life stories, and stories of hope, as glimpsed through the thoughts of Joe's ghost. Excellent characterization, clever points of view. Revelations throughout the telling will surprise you. The story of hope that Sanders has created will grab you and keep you engrossed until the very end."

"Trust me when I saw you won't need a tissue but a whole box, this storyline really tugs at your heart and you won't be the same after reading it. I'm really looking forward to see where book 2 will take me. Give this book a change it's so very worth your time."

Forward

As anyone familiar with Amish culture knows, the rules they live by, also known as the *Ordnung,* prohibits violence against another person. Make no mistake about it, this is an admirable goal. However, being human, situations might occur that make them reconsider it.

I enjoy writing stories that challenge characters like this one does, and what better way to do that than to have one's children taken from them by a "murderer with a savage past?"

Please know, readers, although this story may seem to question Amish values and suggest they not follow them, it is not the case. Going back to my earlier statement, I enjoy writing stories that challenge characters, and that's why I wrote this one like I did.

Some may disagree with, or not know, how some Amish Bishops might only use traditional passages from the Bible, or how they might not suggest others study the Bible, which is mentioned in this story. More than one online resource points both out, which surprised me like it might surprise you. I don't assume to know the reasons, but it does happen. This is not a judgment, but it makes for interesting material for fiction.

Again, in no way am I attempting to judge Amish traditions. In many ways, they are people to be admired, and the world would do well to learn from them.

Thank you for your consideration.

J. Wills Sanders
3/28/2023

The Easter Prayer

Chapter 1

A t the window of their new log cabin, washing supper dishes in the basin, Naomi Ebersole watched Stephen, her husband of ten years, chopping wood. Although April in central Ohio was just around the corner, frost and snow could still linger. This meant they and their children, eight-year-old Timmy and ten-year-old Lucy, needed all the wood they could get for the fireplace on frigid nights.

Living on a new farm created many challenges, especially since the nearest neighbors of their Amish community, Susan and John Yoder, lived an hour away by wagon. The rest formed a rough semicircle around the bishop's home, where they usually met for services, with Naomi and Stephen's farm being the farthest away, near a huge tract of woods known as the Wilderness.

Such was life in 1826, Naomi knew, but she was grateful for each blessing that *Gott* sent her and Stephen, such as Timmy and Lucy.

Susan and John would be similarly blessed anytime now with their first child, and Naomi was taking the wagon there in the morning to see if she could help with the birth. Stephen didn't mind as the local Shawnee tribe had moved further west, lessening the chance of attacks. The main thing to worry about now was wild animals, mainly bears, wolves, and cougars. If one stayed close to home at dusk and dawn, and inside in the dark of night, that risk was minimal too.

With Stephen, Timmy placed a stick of

wood on a second chopping block, raised a pretend ax over his shoulder, and brought it down onto the wood. He knocked the wood off the block as if it had split, then wiped pretend sweat from his forehead, making Naomi smile.

At the table behind her, Lucy was practicing her letters. "D is for dog. D-o-g, dog. T is for Timmy. M-e-a-n, Timmy." She paused. *"Maam,* why is Timmy mean?"

Naomi looked over her shoulder. "He's not mean until you tease him." She knew Lucy meant when Timmy threw her corn shuck doll into the fireplace after she made fun of how he woke this morning with his hair pointing every which way. "He's nice to you otherwise, so stop teasing him."

"Well, it's not the same."

"Your *daat* will make you another doll, so stop complaining and be grateful. You'd miss not having a brother if something happened to him."

Lucy giggled. "Maybe a bear will eat him,

3

or a cougar or a wolf. Or maybe an Indian will take him away."

Washing a heavy cast iron frying pan, Naomi looked over her shoulder again. "I hope you don't mean that. Make sure to ask *Gott* for forgiveness when you say your prayers before bed tonight."

"M is for *maam.* M-e-a-n, *maam.*"

"Be careful, young lady. You're not too old for me to get your britches."

"I wear dresses. You can get Timmy's britches for burning my doll. D is for doll. Doll, d-o-l-l. F is for fire. F-i-r-e, fire."

Naomi whirled around, ready to make her daughter kneel and pray for forgiveness this very instant, but the rattle of a wagon and the whinny of a horse made her open the cabin door.

Their bishop, Levi Miller, climbed down from the wagon. "Stephen, Naomi, might I have a word?"

"Go in the house with Lucy," Naomi told

Timmy.

"What's wrong?" Lucy asked from beside her.

Naomi didn't answer. When she got Timmy and Lucy inside, she closed the door and joined Levi and Stephen beside the wagon. The bishop, normally smiling and waving when he arrived, was obviously bothered by something.

"What is it?" Stephen asked. "You look upset."

"What I am is relieved. I just came from town. Rumor has it that the Shawnee have completely left the Wilderness and are moving west."

Although Naomi didn't put much stock in rumors, if settlers in the area were safer, she was happy. Regardless of Indian attacks, some were friendly, and their plight of having to deal with people invading their lands bothered her. If the proverbial shoe were on the other foot, the settlers might understand them better. At the same time, though, wantonly killing men, women, and children, sometimes kidnapping them, did nothing to make anyone take the time to understand them. It was a complicated matter, one she didn't care to consider. She just prayed for peace on both sides.

"Have you heard anything from Susan and John?" she asked the bishop. "Her time is getting near."

"Not since our last meeting."

"She sure is large," Stephen said.

Naomi heard the concern in his voice. Timmy had been a large baby, making her labor difficult. With the Shawnee gone, the slight concern about the wagon ride in the morning left her.

The bishop touched the wide brim of his black hat. "I just thought I'd share the news. I'll get home and work on my sermon for next Sunday."

As the wagon rattled away, Naomi faced Stephen. "I'm glad we're safer with the

Shawnee gone, but—"

"No buts," Stephen said, cutting her off. "I know you have a soft spot in your heart for their plight, but since they see nothing wrong with killing innocent men, women, and children who just want to live in peace, I'm glad they're gone." Stephen paused. "They're not proud of being called warriors for nothing. I hear some of the different tribes have been warring and enslaving each other for as long as they've existed. Now they're doing it to us. Until they end their ruthless ways, peace isn't possible, whether it be between them and us or between them and themselves."

Concerning this particular part of all the different tribe's stories, Naomi agreed with her intelligent husband. How anyone who fights and enslaves their own people expects peace from anyone else, she didn't know. Then again, she did know—through Jesus's admonition of loving our neighbors like we should love ourselves. Sadly, too many on both sides—Indian and those who hated them—refused Jesus's words of love and wisdom. Until they did, the world would continue to be filled with suffering and heartache.

Stephen kissed her cheek. "I see that troubled look in your eyes. "Yes, I pray for everyone, not just our Amish brethren. Although I pray for all the different tribes, not just the Shawnee, to come to know Jesus, I pray they come to understand how they have no right to kill and kidnap us. Some people in town want to take their children and raise them as *Englisch,* saying they are heathens. Apart from their warring ways, the various tribes live much like the Amish, hunting and tending crops. As long as they don't threaten anyone, who are the *Englisch* to force their ways on them by taking their children?"

Knowing Stephen's question was rhetorical, for they often discussed this topic, Naomi said nothing. All she could do was pray for people to see the errors of their ways so they wouldn't keep repeating them. She decided to lighten the subject. "I look forward to seeing Susan and John. You know I might stay a while if her labor starts while I'm there."

"Of course I know," Stephen said, poking her tummy. "I never thought Timmy would get here when you had him. You sounded like a Shawnee yelling a war whoop." He kissed her temple. "Take as long as you need."

The cabin door opened. Timmy and Lucy came out. "What did the bishop want, *Daat?*" Lucy asked.

"He said the Shawnee have left the Wilderness."

"Good," Timmy said. "You said the biggest turkeys are in the Wilderness, so we can get ours there for Easter supper."

"When will we get some pigs?" Lucy asked. "I like ham better."

J. Willis Sanders

Stephen pointed at the pile of cedar posts beside the chicken coop. "We'll get some pigs when I build the pigpen."

"We had one at our other farm. Why did we have to move?"

"It's not nice to ask so many questions," Timmy said, shoving his sister's shoulder.

She shoved him back. "It's not nice to shove someone."

Stephen scooped Timmy into his arms. "Now, now, you two behave."

"As I was going to say," Naomi said, "we moved to be near our friends instead of near town." She didn't say the rest: *where the drunkards frequent the bawdy house, carrying on until all hours of the night.*

Lucy frowned. "Near our friends? The nearest people are the Yoders, and they don't have any children to play with."

"You liked Timmy when he was a baby," Stephen said, setting his son on his feet. You can play with the Yoder's baby when he or

10

she is born."

Timmy giggled. "And you can change poopy diapers."

"Enough," Naomi said. She faced Stephen. "When do you plan to hunt a turkey? Easter's next weekend, and I'd like to have one for when our community gathers."

"The last time I saw any was when I went deer hunting in the woods. I might try there."

"If I recall correctly, you hiked five miles into the Wilderness for that deer. You were lucky a Shawnee warrior didn't get you."

"Then I'll be doubly lucky now," Stephen said, winking, "since they're gone."

"I thought you said good things happening are blessings?" Lucy asked.

Stephen tapped her nose with a fingertip. "Right you are, Lucy."

"I'm kind of sad the Indians are gone," Timmy said. "Not all of them were bad."

Naomi was grateful for her son's attitude,

11

for too many people held one opinion about the Indians. They were like everyone else: some good, some bad, some in between. Some were downright evil, though. One such ancient Shawnee chief called Black Ears was said to collect the ears of his victims, dry them over a fire until they were black, then string them together as war trophies. No one had ever seen him, so maybe, like with other rumors about Indian atrocities, he was just a rumor.

Stephen and Timmy stacked wood. Naomi and Lucy went inside to stoke the fire for the coming night and to heat water for bathing.

After everyone washed, said their prayers, and climbed into bed—Timmy and Lucy slept in the loft overhead—Naomi blew out the lamp.

As the fire popped and crackled in the fireplace, she prayed again, this time for the health of John and Susan's baby to come, for the men in town to depart their wicked ways, and for the Shawnee to have a safe journey to wherever their new home would be, adding a final word for them to learn to live in peace instead of war, even with other Indian tribes.

Chapter 2

Naomi woke to darkness and an empty bed. She touched Stephen's pillow. Still warm, it likely meant he had dressed and gone to the outhouse. In her nightgown and bare feet, chilled by the cabin floor, she added wood to the embers in the fireplace and stirred them with the poker until flames warmed her face.

The door creaked open; cold air blew in. "Someone will have a cold ride in the wagon this morning," Stephen said. "It's even snowing a little." He came over and knelt behind Naomi. His hands encircled her waist. "How's our new son or daughter this morning?"

"Well," Naomi said, cringing at the touch of his cold hands through the thin material of her nightgown. "No morning sickness for a week is a good sign."

"Are you ready to tell the children?"

"Let's wait until I show. I'd hate to disappoint them with a miscarriage. That's why I wanted to wait the last time."

Stephen stood and helped her up. "I'm glad we did, oh wise wife of mine." He kissed her. "In case I forget to tell you in the hustle and bustle of our daily work, I love you."

Naomi returned the kiss. "I love you too, sweetheart."

Lucy climbed down from the loft. "Why is it so cold?" she asked, rubbing her eyes.

"Look outside and see," Stephen said.

She went to a window. "It's just a little snow and some wind." She shivered. "I don't like wind." In the far corner, a bedsheet up for privacy, she dressed and returned to the living area, wearing a black dress past her knees, a white *kapp*, and a pair of scuffed leather shoes.

Timmy climbed down from the loft and hurried to the corner to dress, then emerged in black pants, a white shirt with black suspenders, and a similar pair of shoes, except his socks were showing.

Naomi sighed. She had let his pants out last month and needed to do so again. Cracking eggs into a bowl, she told the children to go to the henhouse for today's eggs.

While they did, Stephen sliced bacon from a slab of smoked pork. "I look forward to having our own pigs. This bacon cost me more corn than I wanted to trade at the store."

When the bacon sizzled in the cast iron pan, it sent a delicious aroma from the fireplace, where it rested on a metal grate over the glowing embers, pulled to one side for cooking.

The children returned with a basket of eggs. Naomi moved the bacon aside in the huge pan and poured scrambled eggs in.

From behind her, Lucy huffed. "We have no flour, and I wanted biscuits."

"I'll get some in town the next time we go," Stephen said, turning the bacon.

"We need some milk," Timmy said.

"Then go milk the cow," Lucy said.

"Don't boss me."

"Don't whine about milk."

Naomi started to scold them soundly but didn't. Her temper would make her yell, and she didn't care to do that. Instead, she nudged Stephen's arm. "Are they a blessing or a curse?" she whispered.

He chuckled. "They don't like cold mornings like me."

"I heard that," Lucy said.

"I like mornings," Timmy said. "That's the best time for hunting."

"You've never been," Lucy said. "You're just a baby."

"Daat, make her stop."

Stephen stood and faced them. "Do you know why Amish men wear suspenders?"

Timmy giggled. "To hold our pants up."

"No," Stephen said, glaring at Lucy. "We wear suspenders because it would be too tempting to spank teasing daughters with a belt."

Lucy's mouth fell open. "That would hurt."

"Being mean to your brother hurts him."

"He burned my doll."

"You made fun of his hair."

"It's not the same."

Naomi took the pan to the rough-hewn oak table. Battered and charred with use, it was the perfect place to set a hot pan from the fireplace. "Lucy, don't you want your *daat* to make you a new doll?"

"I wouldn't need one if Timmy hadn't burned mine."

Naomi faced Stephen. "I don't like it,

but—"

"Spare the rod, spoil the child."

She jabbed her finger toward the door. "All right, young lady. If you can't mind, go get a switch."

"I wouldn't go that far," Stephen said. "Switches leave welts on legs."

Timmy took a large wooden spatula from an equally large wooden bowl. "This is what you spanked me with last time, *Daat.*"

"I'm sorry," Lucy said to Naomi. "I won't do it again."

"Don't apologize to your *maam,*" Stephen said. "Apologize to your *bruder.*"

Timmy waved the spatula in the air. "I'd rather she got this."

Lucy's lips puckered, likely because she was about to stick her tongue out at Timmy. "I said I'm sorry."

"Because you don't want a spanking," he grumbled.

"Are you sorry for burning my doll?"

"Are you sorry for making fun of my

hair?"

Stephen went to the door and stopped with his hand on the latch. "I'm about to fetch two switches. Would two certain children like to accept their apologies?"

Both nodded, and Naomi smiled. She loved her children, but they could try her patience at times. Thank goodness she and Stephen agreed to discipline them with a firm hand when needed.

At the table, he said the blessing, adding for *Gott* to give Naomi a safe journey to check on Susan today. While they ate, she asked the children if they would like to go with her. Lucy, no doubt, still angry from almost being punished, just shook her head. Timmy said he wanted to stay home in case he and *Daat* went hunting.

In a hurry to leave, Naomi had Lucy wash the dishes. Wearing a woolen black cloak to her knees, she climbed aboard the wagon and thanked Stephen for hitching the mule to it, waved goodbye and snapped the reins.

Although the snow had stopped, gray clouds still hung low in the sky, and the wind managed to whip around her legs and chill her to the bone.

To her right, stretching to the horizon, the Wilderness's huge tract of leafless trees, except for some early budding limbs, resembled skeletal hands protruding from the ground. Here and there they rose on rolling hills and fell to deep hollows shadowed in darkness, where even the rays of the rising sun couldn't reach. Yes, turkey and deer thrived there, which is why Stephen had tracked that deer so far despite the danger of the Shawnee. With them gone, he would hunt there more often. Still, bears, cougars, and wolves were a danger, but at least they, like Black Ears, didn't hunt people just for the sake of killing them and taking their ears.

Lost in thought, Naomi arrived at the fork in the road. The left fork passed Susan and

John's farm and continued to the bishop's home, eventually arriving at town. The right fork continued into the Wilderness. Some said it passed through it; some said it ended deep inside it. Steering the mule to the left fork, Naomi didn't care to find out. The last thing she wanted was to meet Black Ears, rumor or not.

To ease her mind, she silently prayed her favorite Bible verse concerning fear: Psalm 23:1–6. *Yea, though I walk through the valley of the shadow of death, I will fear no evil: for thou art with me; thy rod and thy staff they comfort me.*

Over and over she repeated the prayer. Over and over a chill shook her body, whether from fear or from the frigid wind biting her legs and cheeks, she didn't know.

The mule snorted and his ears waggled. Although no flies buzzed around him, his brown hide rippled.

"Behave, Rufus," Naomi said. "The

Shawnee are gone and the good Lord will keep us safe from anything else."

Rufus looked back at her, huge eyes doubting.

"Don't look at me like that. Have faith, like the Bible says." Naomi rolled her eyes. Here she was, talking to a mule about having faith when hers concerning Black Ears needed to be stronger.

Rufus raised his tail; dark clods of manure dropped to the road. At least he had calmed down enough to do that.

A few minutes away from John and Susan's farm, as Rufus rounded a curve, Naomi's eyes widened. Up ahead, John's horse, Red, was lying in the road, legs kicking. John took his musket from the wagon and aimed it at Red's head. The musket boomed. Black smoke billowed from the barrel; a gust of wind whipped it away. Red's legs stilled.

Nearing the scene, Naomi pulled Rufus's reins, stopping him. "I was just coming to check on Susan, John. What happened to Red?"

John reloaded the musket and returned it to the wagon. "I was in a hurry and let him get too close to the side of the road." He pointed behind him. "He stepped in a groundhog hole and broke his leg. I was coming to get you. Susan started having pains after breakfast."

Naomi could hear the worry in the man's voice. "It can take a day or more, so there's plenty of time yet. Tie your wagon to mine and I'll take you back home."

Standing over Red's body, John shook his head. "I hate to leave Red here like that. It breaks my heart to think of what the buzzards and other animals will do to him." He faced Naomi. "Well, it'll be *Gott's* will."

He connected the wagons and climbed aboard, and Naomi snapped the reins. "Let's go, Rufus. We've got to get this worried *daat* home."

When they arrived at John and Susan's home, a log cabin with a well in front and an outhouse in back, a garden to one side and a henhouse to the other side, he hopped from the wagon and ran inside. Understanding his concern, Naomi steered Rufus to the barn and unhitched him, left him in a stall with water and hay.

Inside the cozy home, similar to her own, with a cooking and living area and a loft, Susan lay in bed, John standing at her side. "Naomi's here, thank *Gott*. It'll be all right now."

Sweat beaded Susan's forehead. "How did you get back so fast?"

"Red stepped in a hole and broke his leg just down the road. Naomi brought me and the wagon back."

"Poor Red," Susan said, her voice filled with sorrow. "He was a fine horse with a gentle temper. I'll miss him."

"We'll get another soon," John said. "How are your pains now?"

Susan answered by gritting her teeth.

"How far apart are they?" Naomi asked.

Susan's tight expression relaxed. "A little less than fifteen minutes."

Naomi patted her hand. "Well, this is your first baby. It can take quite a while."

"Thank you for coming," Susan said, offering a weak smile. "I'm sure Stephen and the children need you at home."

After offering John a grin, Naomi smiled at Susan. "Oh, I know how our menfolk depend on us. He and the children will just have to depend on themselves for a while."

Chapter 3

About to start digging the holes for the cedar posts to make the pigpen, Stephen stuck the shovel in the ground and took the dress from Lucy. "I don't see a hole."

"It's under the arm, *Daat.* Can you mend it?"

"Don't you know how? I see you sewing with your *maam* all the time."

"She makes a special stitch there. She hasn't taught me yet."

Beside her, Timmy giggled. "Your stinky underarms made a hole in your dress."

Stephen eyed his son. "I know a certain boy who has stinky underarms too."

"That's cause I do a man's work. *Maam*

27

and Lucy just do women's work."

Lucy glared at him. "I'll remember that if *Maam* doesn't come home tonight and you want me to cook supper. You can eat rocks instead of biscuits."

"Your biscuits *are* like rocks."

"Now, Son," Stephen said, interceding to head off the argument before it got worse. "Your sister baked the biscuits too long that one time. From then on they've been as good as your *maam's*."

"But—"

"No buts. Be grateful for Lucy. Remember the Bible verse I taught you from First Thessalonians? 'Rejoice always, pray without ceasing, give thanks in all circumstances; for this is the will of *Gott* in Christ Jesus for you.'"

Timmy frowned. "You mean I gotta be thankful for hard biscuits?"

"We ate them. Would you rather never have any biscuits?"

"I guess not." Timmy faced Lucy. "I'm sorry." He grinned. "You really don't stink. Me and *Daat* do stink after we work."

Lucy offered him the dress. "Maybe you can wear this and make biscuits so you don't stink."

All three burst out laughing, making Stephen proud of his children for learning to appreciate each other. As he pulled the shovel from the ground and started digging the first post hole, Timmy pointed. *"Daat!* I see some turkeys by the woods!"

Stephen turned toward the Wilderness. By the edge of the woods, in the field he had plowed to plant corn, two hen turkeys pecked at the soil. One gobbler, a long beard hanging from its throat, strutted and spread his tail and gobbled.

Stephen gave Timmy the shovel. "Keep digging, Son. I'll get my musket and see if I can get that gobbler."

Inside, he grabbed the musket from over the fireplace, plus powder and shot, and rejoined the children. "I need to hike down the field and cut into the woods to sneak up on those turkeys. It might take a while. If I'm not back soon, have lunch without me."

"I need my dress mended," Lucy said, watching *Daat* leave. "It's my best one. I want to wear it to our Easter supper."

Timmy set the shovel on the ground and tried digging with it by pressing it into the hard sod with his foot. "Ugh, this is hard work." He leaned the shovel against the stack of cedar poles. "I guess we have to wait until *Maam* and *Daat* get back to get anything done around here."

Lucy didn't like waiting. She wanted her dress fixed in case any of the boys paid her any attention. Ten was too young to court, but she wanted to make a good impression for when she got older. Inside, she left a note for *Daat* on the table, saying she was taking the dress to the Yoders for *Maam* to mend. Donning her long, black cloak and black bonnet over her white *kapp,* she faced Timmy. "I'm going to the Yoders. Do you want to go or stay here. It's not that far."

"Do you remember which fork to take in the road?"

Lucy tapped her lips with a fingertip. "I think it's the right fork. It's been a while since we all went there."

Timmy nodded. "I think it's the right fork too. The other one goes into the Wilderness. I'm glad the Shawnee are gone. That wouldn't be a good place to go if they were still there." He donned his black coat and pressed his wide-brimmed straw hat down on his head. *"Daat's* not here. I'm the man of the house. I better go with you."

Outside, as they set off down the dirt road, Lucy shaded her eyes. "I don't see *Daat* or the turkeys. He must be after them in the woods."

Timmy licked his lips. "I love roasted turkey with giblet gravy and stuffing."

Lucy glanced at him. "It's good, but I like

31

ham better."

"You can always stay home and dig those holes for those cedar posts. Then we can get some pigs."

Lucy said nothing. Despite all the arguing with her *bruder*, she loved him, but he sure could be silly at times. He was stouter than her. If he couldn't dig a hole, she couldn't either.

* * *

Astride his horse atop one of the rolling hills within the Wilderness, warmed by buckskin pants, a shirt, and moccasins, Black Ears lowered the spy glass. He had taken it from the body of a red-coat soldier many years ago, when the Shawnee fought with the Virginians against the British. Now he was reduced to a chief without a tribe.

Although his people had traveled west, the last thing on earth he would do was to run away like a coward from the land of his birth. Yes, he might be forced to do so one day, but he planned to send as many settlers to their graves as possible first. Being a warrior demanded it, both now and in the past, when his people fought the Iroquois. Many a warrior had died by his arrows. Many a woman had been taken into slavery. Many a child had been sold to other tribes. Black Ear's blood lusted for the blood of his enemies even more now than then, and he had his pick of settlers to choose from. Now, though, instead of fighting for his people, he would fight for himself, betrayed by the Americans he had fought with against the British.

He raised the spy glass again. Not only had one possible victim taken a wagon along the road this morning, another had entered the Wilderness to hunt three turkeys, and two more now walked the road, the children of the other two.

Black Ears lowered the spy glass. These strange people didn't seem afraid of anything, for they started moving near the

Wilderness before the Shawnee left, building houses and barns and chicken coops and pigpens and fences for their cows, mules, and horses. Anytime in the day, they might stop working and bow their heads. Black Ears wondered if they had stiff necks from all their work, and they bowed their heads to loosen their necks.

Along with that strange action, they wore clothes unlike those of the people in town. When they gathered at various homes, they reminded him of a flock of crows, black dresses and pants legs flapping in a breeze. The men wore hats of woven straw. The women wore black hats that wrapped around their heads and hooded their faces. At home, however, they wore much smaller hats, white instead of black, that did not hood their faces. Black Ears couldn't figure them out, but he might soon see if they bled and died like other people did. As far as the children, like the boy and girl walking the road now, they might fetch a good trade with whatever tribes he might find on the path to the west. Yes, he would leave and find his people, but only after he had enacted his revenge.

He paused in his thoughts.

A better revenge would be to take these two children and know their mother and father and all the people who gathered at the various homes would agonize over what had happened to them. After all, the same thing had happened to him while he fought with the Virginians against the British, when the Iroquois snuck into his tribe's camp and killed his wife and took his children. By the time he found the Iroquois and killed the small band of warriors, the last one, dying with a spear in his chest, had laughed about how they had traded Black Ear's children to another group of Iroquois and watched them torture them.

He took a piece of smoked venison from a leather bag slung over his shoulder and chewed it.

From time to time over the years, the Shawnee elders had gathered to discuss important matters. Along with what to do about the Europeans spreading everywhere, they questioned why so many tribes warred against each other as they always seem to have done. Like with the Shawnee and the Iroquois, word came from the west, where the Comanche and the Apache not only fought each other, they fought the Pueblos. Endless wars made no sense. Even the Europeans warred, like with the Americans and the British and the French.

What spark of goodness all mankind lacked that made them do such things, Black Ears didn't know. He prayed often to the Great Spirit about it, especially his desire to kill settlers and kidnap children.

On occasion, a twinge of guilt entered his heart. When this happened, he scoffed at it, thinking it was because his children had suffered the same fate from the Iroquois. But at other times, as he aimed an arrow at a man or woman, the fear in their eyes and the screams from their throats reminded him of how his wife and children must have screamed during their ordeals.

Black Ears washed the venison down with water from a skin, tied the opening and returned it to the leather bag. *Enough*, he thought. Thinking of his wife and children would only weaken his resolve for revenge.

He raised the spy glass once more. The children were nearing the fork in the road. Perhaps the Great Spirit would lead them into the Wilderness. If so, they would walk right into his hands. If not, he would need to gallop down the hill and capture them before they rounded the curve out of view and neared the cabin of the next settlers, where the man's musket would be a problem.

The spy glass's metal eyepiece pressed

into Black Ear's brow. He licked his lips in anticipation. His blood pulsed in his temples, like the war drums of his once proud tribe.

The children neared the curve. With his free hand, he gripped the reins. With his feet firmly in the stirrups, he waited to heel the horse's flanks. He felt young again: a warrior ready to do battle, even if only against two small children. Then he smiled as they took the right fork toward his lair, the Wilderness.

Relaxing, he ate more venison. Although he wanted to capture and trade these children, the most important thing was their parent's grief. Let them enter the woods. Let them lose their way. Let them meet a bear, a wolf, or a cougar, or let them starve to death; the result would be the same.

Water followed the venison. The horse snorted. Black Ears steered it down the hill and into a hollow to a creek. The horse noisily sucked water. Black Ears dismounted to fill his skin and to make water. Astride the horse again, he rode to the next hill toward the road. With the spy glass, he caught glimpses of the children through the trees. No doubt they thought they were going to the next cabin, where their mother had gone. Although the road would end far inside the Wilderness, they might realize they had taken the wrong fork before then. If so, and if they turned back, he would ride down and tie their wrists with leather thongs and lead them to his camp. Then he would get them on his other horse and start west.

Chapter 4

Lucy trudged along the dusty road. It hadn't rained recently, and her and Timmy's shoes left only the hints of prints in the hard soil.

"I thought we would be there by now," Timmy said.

Lucy said nothing. She thought so too, and she was sure they had taken the correct fork. "I think it takes longer."

The first part of the road took them through *Daat's* fields. After the fork, trees gradually enclosed them, darkening everything around them. Everywhere Lucy looked, she could imagine the slitted yellow eyes of either wolves, cougars, or bears peeking at her and Timmy from behind trees. Fangs gleamed. Claws glistened. Lips were licked. Fear roiled in her stomach.

Timmy jerked to a stop. "What's that noise in the woods?"

Intent on her thoughts, Lucy hadn't heard anything. "Where?"

Timmy pointed. "In the trees behind us. I heard leaves crunching."

"Maybe it's a squirrel."

Behind them, on the side of the road, a clump of brush shook, and Timmy picked up a rock. "That's too much shaking for a squirrel."

A rabbit burst from the brush and ran across the road, and Timmy dropped the rock, laughing. "It's just a cottontail."

To their left, something else crunched the leaves as if it were running and leaping through the woods, and Lucy recognized the sleek gray form of a wolf. "Hold still," she whispered to Timmy. "A wolf is chasing that rabbit and we want it to *keep* chasing it."

The wolf came closer. Fear chilled the nape of Lucy's neck. Timmy stood stock still. His and Lucy's breaths made little puffs of white in the cold air. They were upwind of the wolf, and she could smell it, the same as a dog they'd once had.

It leapt into the road and stopped. The black nose raised to sniff the air, then lowered to the road. Lucy prayed for the breeze to not shift.

Still sniffing the road, the wolf crept across the road and continued into the woods.

Lucy relaxed. Timmy sighed in relief, evidenced by a huge puff of white from his mouth. They turned to continue down the road, and Lucy felt the breeze shift from the nape of her neck to her face.

In the woods, a growl erupted from the wolf's throat. As Timmy picked up the rock again, his hand shaking, she grabbed his arm. "See that tree with the low limbs?"

Not needing any more prompting, Timmy dropped the rock and ran to the tree, Lucy on his heels.

The wolf growled again, followed by a howl. From deep in the woods, in the direction it had come from, several howls answered.

Lucy and Timmy scampered up the tree. Brush and leaves crunched behind them. She looked down in time to see the wolf leaping for her foot, which she jerked away as his teeth grazed her shoe. Higher they climbed, until the wolf couldn't reach them. Standing on a limb, Timmy wrapped his arms around the trunk. "You just had to fix your silly dress, didn't you? And you even forgot the stupid thing."

Lucy gaped. Like her *bruder* had said, she'd left the dress at home. "Well, you *let* me leave it."

"I knew you left it. I thought it would be funny when you noticed." Timmy looked down at the leaping wolf. "It isn't funny now. All this because you wanted to look good for the boys."

"Shut up. At least those other wolves aren't coming."

The wolf stopped leaping. It raised its nose and howled again, this time long, loud, and quavering.

Please, Gott, Lucy prayed. *Don't let those other wolves come.*

Timmy shoved her arm. "Listen."

From behind them, deep within the woods, leaps and bounds matched the crunching leaves. The pack was coming.

Lucy stopped praying and opened her eyes. "We're safe up here, but …"

"But what?" Timmy asked, looking up from the wolf.

"When *Daat* gets back from hunting, he'll read the note and think we're with *Maam.*"

"And she thinks we're with him." Timmy's mouth fell open. "We might have to stay here until Mrs. Yoder has her baby.

How long does that take?"

"You don't want to know," Lucy said.

"An hour?"

"She said it took me all day and night."

"We'll freeze up here at night."

Growls and crunching leaves made them look down. The pack had joined the other wolf, and they all looked up at their possible supper. Eyes narrowed. Tongues licked lips. Teeth were bared.

Lucy faced Timmy. "I'd rather freeze then be eaten."

Timmy smacked the tree's trunk. "You and your stupid dress."

"Shut up."

"*You* shut up."

At the base of the tree, the largest wolf leaped, almost reaching the lowest branch. If it gained that one, it could climb the rest.

"Pray, Timmy," Lucy hissed. "Pray hard!"

The wolf leaped again and pulled itself onto the branch. Baring its teeth in what resembled a wicked grin, it gathered itself for another leap—and fell amongst the pack of wolves, an arrow in its side. What sounded like a horse's hooves came from a thicket. The wolves scattered as an Indian rode up and drew rein.

Lucy didn't know what to think. The Indian wore buckskins. Sweat stained the underarms. Dark hair, mixed with gray, hung down his back. He wore a red bandana around his head. Wrinkles creased his face. He slung a bow over his shoulder, alongside a quiver full of arrows, and looked up. "I think you are lost. If you come down, I'll get you a horse so you can ride home."

"How … how do you know where we live?" Timmy asked, his voice filled with fear.

"I know everything. These are my woods and my animals. I watch your people all the time. Why do you gather at your houses in

46

large groups?"

"We're Amish," Lucy said. "We meet to worship *Gott.*"

The Indian grunted. "Come down." He brought a leg over the horse's back and slid to the ground, moving with surprising grace to be so old. "You're safe now." He pulled the arrow from the wolf, wiped the stone tip on a handful of leaves, and returned it to the quiver.

"I don't think we should," Timmy whispered to Lucy. "He might be Black Ears."

Lucy held in a gasp. The name of Black Ears had spread fear amongst both the townspeople and the Amish. Despite that fear, their faith in *Gott* had set it aside in order to be together as a community.

She peered down at him. "Are you Shawnee or Iroquois?"

"I am Shawnee. The Iroquois are my enemy, like they were your enemy in the war many years ago. I fought with the

Virginians against the red-coat British. I am not your enemy."

Lucy nodded. That must be how this man had learned to speak English so well. "What's your name?"

"What is *your* name? I saved you from the wolves. Do not be rude."

"I'm Timmy," Timmy said. "How many British did you kill?"

"More than you can count."

"The Amish don't believe in violence," Lucy said.

The Shawnee chuckled. "Do you believe in letting wolves eat you?"

"I mean violence against people."

"My people fought and died to free your people from the British. That you Amish would not is an insult. You are cowards." The Shawnee took a deep breath. "Are you coming down or not? I do not have all day."

Lucy was still afraid this Shawnee was Black Ears. "I'm Lucy. Tell us your name first."

"You are more trouble than you are worth. Maybe I should leave and let the wolves come back."

Timmy snorted laughter. "What kind of Shawnee is afraid to tell his name?"

Like a man trying to think of something, the Shawnee looked away and back, pursing his lips. "I am Quick Arrow." He nudged the wolf with the toe of his moccasin. "As you can see."

"Do you have a family?" Lucy asked.

Quick Arrow's jaw tensed. "That is not your concern."

"I think he just made that name up," Timmy whispered to Lucy. "I think he's Black Ears."

"Black Ears would've killed us instead of that wolf," Lucy whispered back. "I want to go home. No one will come looking for us until *Maam* comes home or *Daat* goes to the Yoders. We'll freeze if we stay out here."

"We don't need a horse to get home. Why

does he want to put us on a horse?"

"The road curves a lot. Maybe we're farther from home than it seems."

Off in the distance, the wolf pack howled.

"Perhaps I should leave and let them have you," Quick Arrow said. "Anyone who ignores help is a fool. Maybe the wolves will leave some bones for your mother and father to find."

At the thought of what Quick Arrow suggested, Lucy faced Timmy. "We better go down. We'll know soon enough if he's lying."

They eased down the tree, taking care not to land on the dead wolf when they jumped from the last limb.

"You are very smart," Quick Arrow said. "Follow me. I'll have you home soon." He heeled the horse and started up the slight hill.

Beside Lucy, Timmy looked at her. "I don't like this."

At least he didn't say it was because of her dress. "I don't like it either, but it's better than freezing to death or wolves eating us. Even if we try walking back home, they might come after us again."

As they crunched through leaves, splashed through creeks, climbed hills, and walked around dead trees in some of the hollows, Lucy wondered what *Maam* and *Daat* were doing. Thank *Gott* they weren't following a Shawnee to his camp, where who knew what might happen.

Chapter 5

Almost home from his two-hour hunt, Stephen moved the heavy gobbler to his other shoulder, aching from the weight. What a meal it would make for the Easter supper, when everyone gathered this Sunday.

Passing the pile of cedar poles, he noticed the shovel leaning against them. The ground was hard, but Timmy should've given it more of an effort than a few marks in the dirt. He left the turkey by the door.

Inside, about to call the children, he raised the note on the table. It was only a few miles to the Yoders, so they should be all right. Might as well pluck that turkey and get it soaking in cold water in the ice house.

As he snatched feathers, a touch of worry tightened his lips. Yes, the Shawnee had gone west, but did anyone say they *all* had gone west? All it took was one malcontent to take the lives of several people—a malcontent like Black Ears.

When the community members started moving here from town, the Shawnee had ignored them. They were known for fighting with the Virginians against the British in the war of independence, so maybe they held no ill will toward today's Americans. They also were known for fighting the Iroquois, so no one really knew what kind of ill will they held toward anyone. Past stories said most tribes, regardless of name or location, were capable of anything. Stephen couldn't imagine settlers having their children taken and sold to a tribe for whatever reason, and he didn't care to try. Like with Africans brought here as slaves, being taken from a home and placed in a strange land was wrong, no matter who the victims were.

Done plucking the turkey, he drew water from the well to fill a large basin he had taken to the ice house, eased the bird into it, and went to wash the tiny pin feathers from his hands.

Drying them by the door, he checked the location of the sun, now lowering from the midday sky. The children would likely stay with their *Maam* instead of risking a twilight walk with wild animals roaming the Wilderness. Thank goodness no one had to worry about the Shawnee being there anymore.

* * *

Tired from tromping through woods, climbing hills, and sliding down hollows on slippery leaves, Lucy stopped. "How much farther is it? I'm tired."

Quick Arrow looked over his shoulder.

54

"You would never make a Shawnee wife. They are strong."

"I don't want to be a Shawnee wife. All I want is to go home."

"Then stop complaining and walk."

Timmy leaned close to Lucy. "I don't remember all these woods on the way to the Yoder's house," he whispered. "I think we're in the Wilderness."

Lucy was beginning to think the same thing. "If we took the wrong fork, Quick Arrow—if that's his name—could've walked us home by the road."

Quick Arrow stopped the horse and slid off the saddle. "I am old, but my ears are good," he said, his voice hard. "I am Black Ears, and you are my prisoners. You will never go home again."

Lucy's knees gave way; she fell in the leaves. *Gott,* she prayed, *please give Timmy and me the strength to get through this.*

Timmy kicked Black Ears' shin. "Run, Lucy!"

Before Lucy could rise, Black Ears backhanded Timmy across the face, and her brother fell. Pressing a hand to his cheek, he glared up at Black Ears. "You're an evil man. Leave us alone."

Lucy rose from her knees. "The Amish haven't done anything to the Shawnee. We believe in peace, not violence."

Black Ears rubbed his shin. "You lie. All whites lie. You have no honor." He took two lengths of rawhide from his pocket. "I have a horse for you at camp. You can ride it with your wrists tied or not. Which will it be?"

"Where are you taking us?" Lucy asked, imagining the worst but praying for *Gott* to intervene.

"You will know when we get there." He rubbed his shin again. "I'll tie you at night. Your brother might try to kill me."

Timmy clenched his jaw: an angry boy who had forgotten his Amish teachings. Lucy didn't blame him, but she had been taught to forgive. Regardless, she wanted to go home. If they bided their time, maybe they could talk at night and make a plan.

Standing upright to make herself look tall, she straightened her black bonnet and looked Black Ears straight in his dark eyes. "I don't want to fall off a horse, so you don't need to tie us." She faced Timmy, whose cheek was reddening. "Okay?" He nodded but said nothing.

Now wary that they might run, no doubt, Black Ears motioned them forward and followed them on foot. Minutes later, they approached a barely smoldering fire with a deer haunch hanging over it. A small structure made from deer hides served as Black Ears' shelter. Another horse was tied to a tree.

Black Ears threw a saddle blanket and a saddle on the horse, cut the deer haunch into strips and packed them into a rawhide bag from the structure. Then he tied the bag to the saddle. After kicking dirt over the fire, he drank from a skin and it to Lucy. "Drink."

Lucy couldn't stand the thought of pressing her lips where his had pressed, but she did, if only to maintain her strength for a chance at escape.

She offered the skin to Timmy, and he frowned. "I'd rather drink horse urine."

"That can be arranged," Black Ears said.

"Drink," Lucy said, shoving the skin toward her brother again. "*Daat* and *Maam* would want us to take care of ourselves."

Timmy drank and returned the skin to Black Ears. "My *daat* has a musket. I hope he find us and shoots you."

Black Ears removed the deer hides from a framework of curved branches stuck in the ground, rolled them into a bundle and tied it behind his saddle. "Which is why we are leaving now. Get on that horse before I throw you on it."

Not wanting him to touch her, Lucy

climbed into the saddle. She reached down for Timmy's hand and helped him up. At least the horse was short. If they fell, it wouldn't be far to the ground.

Black Ears used his lariat to tie the horses together. Then he climbed into his saddle, heeled the horse's flanks, and they started west, toward the setting sun.

"What are we going to do?" Timmy whispered from behind Lucy. "*Daat* thinks we're with *Maam*, so they won't miss us unless he goes to the Yoders or she goes home."

"We'll try to get away at night."

"What about the wolves?"

"We'll have to take that chance."

Not looking back at them, Black Ears snapped his fingers. "Your whispers aren't much quieter than that. Since you plan to escape at night, I'll tie you to a tree and make you hold your water until I get up."

Timmy pressed harder into Lucy's back. "I hope *Daat* finds us and kills him," he hissed, trying to whisper more quietly.

"He won't," Lucy said, also trying to whisper more quietly. Apparently it worked, for Black Ears ignored them. "You know the Amish don't kill people," she added.

"Not even to save their children from someone like Black Ears?"

"Not that I know of. Maybe *Daat* will get the sheriff to find us."

"Good," Timmy said. "I hope he shoots Black Ears. If not, he'll just get away and take someone else's children."

Lucy understood Timmy. If Black Ears had taken her children, she would have to shoot him. Although evil people couldn't be allowed to harm good people, the ideal was to pray for evil people to realize the errors of their ways and to ask forgiveness from *Gott*. If not, evil people would rule the world. She had heard *Maam* and *Daat* talking about why they moved away from town, and their words about drunkards and the bawdy house proved evil was everywhere. No good came from such things. If it flourished, the fledgling country of America, created from the ideals of liberty, would eventually perish.

The afternoon dragged on. Leaves crunched beneath the horse's hooves, releasing their tangy aroma. A breeze brought the musky odor of a skunk. Time passed with the continuous jostling in the saddle, when the horse stepped over dead trees, crossed creeks, or climbed hills.

Black Ears never looked back, never asked if they were thirsty or hungry or needed to relieve themselves. Lucy's bladder began to ache. She didn't dare ask, afraid he might watch her. Timmy said nothing about it, possibly feeling the same ache and the same fear.

Timmy pressed against her back. "The woods are ending."

Black Ears stopped and pointed. "We are

far away from your people. We'll camp here for the night." He slid off his horse, stepped to a tree to make water, and returned. "See how I turned my back? I am not so bad as you think I am." In turn, he lifted them from the horse and set them down. "Will you run if I untie you so you can make water?"

Timmy scowled at him. "You'd only run us down on your horse."

"Very true. I am glad you see trying to escape is useless." He untied their wrists. "Go do your business and come back. There are plenty of leaves if you need them. Then gather wood for a fire. It will be cold tonight, and I do not want you to freeze."

On the way to a large oak, Lucy's shoes rustled the leaves. While she squatted, Timmy stood on the other side of the wide trunk. "I wonder where he's taking us?"

Done, Lucy stood. "It can't be good, wherever it is."

They traded places. Timmy's pants

rustled as he opened his fly. "Maybe we can kill him when he goes to sleep."

Such a thing shocked Lucy. "Could you really kill someone that easy?"

"It's him or us. Don't you know that?"

"I suppose."

Timmy stepped from behind the tree, a large rock in his hand. "We could do it with this."

The imagined sight of a man's brains bashed out sent a clot of nausea into Lucy's throat. "I—" She swallowed. "I can't do that."

"Not even to save our lives?" Timmy asked, his tone incredulous.

"I don't think so."

He dropped the rock. "You know there are worse things than dying, don't you?"

"No. When we die, we join *Gott* in Heaven."

"I mean before that. One of the boys at school told me what those drunkards do in the bawdy house. You're a girl. Black Ears might take us to men who'll do that to you. I can't stand the thought of it. I'll kill him first."

The clot of nausea rose to Lucy's throat again. *Maam* had explained such things to her upon seeing farm animals doing them. Maybe she could kill to stop anyone from doing that to her.

Black Ears pointed at a circle of rocks he had gathered. "Do like I say and get that wood."

Lucy leaned over to pick up a limb. "We better do what he says." She didn't say the rest: *before he does to me what those men in the bawdy house do to those women.*

They gathered armfuls of branches and took them to the circle of rocks. Using a match, likely stolen from some dead person, Black Ears started a fire. When the embers glowed, he pierced pieces of the deer haunch with green sticks cut from a tree branch and leaned them over the circle of rocks to cook.

Toward the west, the sky transformed from blue to yellow to orange. Finally, except for the circle of light from the embers, darkness engulfed the woods.

What little fat the deer meat held sizzled, sending the enticing aroma to Lucy's nostrils. Timmy licked his lips, reached for his piece, and Black Ears grunted that it wasn't ready. While they waited, he took a pouch from the bag he kept slung over his shoulder, tamped a clay pipe with what must be tobacco, and lit it with a stick from the fire. Puffing, he hummed a soft song of some kind.

"What's that?" Timmy asked. "The song of your dishonor at kidnapping two helpless children?"

Lucy wanted to nudge his knee with hers to shut him up. It made no sense to antagonize this evil Shawnee.

Black Ears chuckled and stopped puffing. "You know nothing of honor. My tribe earned honor time and time again by invading the Iroquois. We left old men and women crying and babies dead."

Lucy was afraid to ask what they did with the younger Iroquois.

Timmy's eyes reflected the glowing embers, red and shining. "Hell holds a special place for people like you, Black Ears. Everything you did to other people will be done to you throughout eternity."

"You claim to know much for one so young, boy."

An idea popped into Lucy's mind. If Black Ears knew their names, he might think of them as people instead of two children to do with as he pleased. "I'm Lucy and my brother is Timmy. Our *maam* and *daat* are Naomi and Stephen Ebersole."

Timmy eyed her, obviously upset by her sharing their names.

Puffing the pipe, Black Ears stopped. "You names do not matter to me. All that matters is you are my prisoners." He motioned to the sizzling meat. "Eat. We will travel far tomorrow. I do not want you falling from the saddle."

Timmy gnawed at the meat, chewed and swallowed a morsel, and faced Black Ears. "What about vegetables and bread?"

Black Ears ignored him, yet his hard, dark eyes shared his opinion of prisoners making requests.

When they finished eating, he offered them water, saying not to drink too much because, like he had already told them, he would tie their wrists for the night and tie them to a tree. This ruined any chances of escape or killing him.

He bound their wrists and ran his lariat through their hands, tied both ends to a tree and added wood to the fire. "Lie close and turn over often, or you won't sleep for the cold."

Lucy lay on her side and faced the fire. Timmy lay at her front with his head by her head. Her cloak and his coat should keep them from getting too cold.

Black Ears used the bundle of deer hides for a bed and a blanket. In turn, his dark eyes focused on each of them until they closed.

In the distance, an owl hooted. In the woods, leaves crunched. Beyond the circle of fire, two slitted eyes glowed, blinked, and went black again as whatever animal it was left a trail of crunching leaves in its wake.

Lucy prayed and prayed and prayed. She hoped Timmy was praying too, for they needed all the help they could get from their Heavenly Father. Eventually she grew drowsy, but burning tears delayed sleep.

The fire's warmth offered solace, the stars too. She wondered if Susan had a new son or daughter yet, wondered if she and Timmy would live to have their own families, and then her eyes finally closed.

Chapter 6

To be ready for the birth of Susan's infant, Naomi drew a pail of water from the well.

Pacing outside the cabin door, John wrung his hands as she approached him. "I'm sorry, Naomi, I should've done that." He opened the door, took the pail from her, and followed her inside. "I suppose we should boil this, yes?"

"That's exactly right," Naomi said, feeling sympathy for this *daat* to be. She went to Susan, who panted in pain every ten minutes or so, and wiped sweat from her brow. "There, there, you're doing fine."

Susan stopped panting. "Please tell me it doesn't get worse."

"I'm afraid it will, but that's the burden we mothers bear." She offered a conspiratorial smile. "A burden men would fail every time, truth be known."

"The pains seem to be coming closer."

"I've been keeping track with the clock on your fireplace mantel. They're between ten and fifteen minutes apart."

"They feel quicker. How long did your first baby take?"

Naomi didn't care to tell Susan the truth, but she needed to know what to expect. "Lucy took seventeen hours and Timmy took fourteen."

"You mean they don't take as long after the first?"

"That's right."

"I suppose that's something."

John came over. "Can I do anything before I walk a trench in the dirt outside the door?"

"You could heat the stew from last night

for supper," Susan said. "Or haven't you noticed it's getting dark?"

"My apologies," Naomi. "I'll do just that."

Susan's calm expression tensed. A groan erupted from her throat. Naomi gripped her hand. "Deep breaths, Susan, deep breaths."

Like earlier, Susan panted until her face finally relaxed. "John Yoder," she said, pointing at him by the fireplace, "I'm not sure if I want any more children or not."

Naomi laughed. "I told Stephen that when Lucy was on the way, but I forgot the pain when I held her in my arms the first time."

The aroma of beef and chicken stew soon made Naomi lick her lips. Some midwives forbade mothers in labor from eating, but she believed a light meal helped keep the strength up. She asked John to bring her and Susan a bowl each. After he said a short blessing, he ate his at the oak table in the kitchen area, a glowing oil lamp

71

illuminating his blue eyes, straight nose, and dark beard. As Naomi suggested, Susan took a few bites and a few sips of water between pains.

Done with her bowl, Naomi washed and dried the dishes and told John she wanted some air. Outside, watching the stars, she missed Stephen and her boisterous children. Yes, they could argue terribly, but she loved them more than she thought possible.

From deep within the Wilderness, a wolf howled, sending a chill along the nape of her neck. Several more quavering voices joined in, creating a lonely, hollow feeling in the pit of her stomach, the same feeling as when she had miscarried her first baby. Thank *Gott* she hadn't lost anymore. Soon, if things went well with the tiny seed of life within in her womb, she and Stephen would be blessed with a brother or sister for John and Lucy.

Inside again, she nodded off and on

throughout the night in a rocking chair, giving John and Susan the privacy of their bed. Toward dawn, signaled by the hazy glow of orange sunlight entering the window, she woke to the smell and sizzle of bacon frying. Kneeling by the fireplace, turning a strip of bacon, John looked over his shoulder when the rocking chair creaked with Naomi's rising. "Susan's water broke an hour ago and her pains are getting closer. She's been clenching her teeth on a piece of leather to keep from waking you."

Susan's kindness touched Naomi. She went to check on her, sleeping at the moment, and returned to the table, where John had plated eggs and bacon and poured coffee. They sat, and he bowed his head.

"Dear Lord, please bless this food for the nourishment of our bodies. Thank you for all your blessings, and please allow Susan and our child to come through the birth well and safe. Amen."

Naomi sipped the delicious coffee.

Despite the heat from the fireplace, it didn't spread around the room, so she enjoyed the steam from the coffee warming her face against the chilly morning.

Behind her, Susan moaned, so Naomi quickly ate while she had time. Apparently sensing the same thing, John wolfed down his food, took the dishes to the basin, and joined Naomi at the bedside.

Susan grimaced. Her eyelids fluttered open. Naomi supported her as she leaned forward and moaned. Five minutes later she did the same thing. Thirty minutes later, five minutes shortened to three, and less than an hour later, Naomi had tied and cut the cord and was placing John and Susan's son in her arms.

"Praise *Gott*," John said, wiping tears. "We have a healthy son."

Susan looked up at him. "We're truly blessed." She squeezed Naomi's hand. "Thank you so much. If he had been a girl, I was going to name her after you."

John snapped his fingers. "I haven't thought of a name."

"I like Timmy," Susan said, "but Naomi and Stephen have a Timmy."

Naomi laughed. "Believe me, one troublesome boy with that name is enough."

"We'll figure it out," John said, touching his son's head.

The infant snuffled against Susan's nightgown. "Uh-oh," she said. "I think someone's hungry."

To give the family privacy, Naomi washed and dried the dishes. The sweet scene behind her made her long to return to her own family. Thank *Gott* her community had left the outskirts of town and moved into the countryside. How anyone could live where men drank and cursed and fought in the one bar before staggering to the bawdy house, she didn't know. Regardless, all she could do was pray for them to understand how their lives were meant for more than those things, which would eventually kill them with diseases of both the body and the mind.

John went outside with the bucket that held the afterbirth and came back. "Brrr, it's cold out there. Spring is taking its time in coming." Warming his hands by the fire, he faced Naomi. "Would you like me to hitch your mule to the wagon so you can go home, or do you want to wait until it gets warmer?"

"Would you like to use him to move Red further off the road?"

"I would, thank you. I'll do it now." A cold blast of air came in when John went out.

Naomi joined Susan. Asleep, the baby lay in the curve of her arm. "Have you thought of a name yet?"

Susan kissed her son's head. "If John likes it, I was thinking of John Jr." She kissed the baby's head again. "How old is Timmy now?"

"He's eight," Naomi said, sitting on the bed.

"Do you think you'll have anymore?"

Naomi pressed her hand to her tummy and smiled. "If *Gott* sees fit, in nine months."

Susan clasped her hand. "That's wonderful. Maybe you'll have another girl, and John Jr. will court her one day."

The idea appealed to Naomi. "I'd like that. Are you hungry? There's some leftover eggs and bacon, and I can warm the coffee."

"You were reading my mind." Susan eased out of bed and put John Jr. in a crib. "Let me visit the outhouse. I'll be right back."

When she returned, Naomi had everything ready, including a cup of coffee for herself. "This is the first time I spent the night away from home since Stephen and I were married."

Susan crunched bacon and swallowed. "I look forward to the community Easter dinner."

"Me too," Naomi said, "especially the cooking of the elder ladies. I can't seem to get my fried chicken to turn out like theirs."

"Nor my green beans. I add pork for seasoning, but it's not the same." Susan forked eggs.

Outside, the rattle of the wagon came from down the road. Minutes later, John came in. "Well, old Red is in the woods. I need to find another horse in town now."

He poured coffee and sat. "Thank you for all your help, Naomi. If I can help with anything, just let me know."

Drinking the last of her coffee, Naomi lowered the cup. "Are you good at tracking? Stephen wants to get a turkey for the Easter meal, and they run into the Wilderness before he can get a gobbler."

John winked at Susan. "Should I tell her?"

78

Susan's lips tightened as she swallowed eggs. "Don't make me laugh while I'm eating," she squeaked.

"I don't understand," Naomi said, eyeing them in turn.

"My grandfather was Shawnee," John said. "Haven't you wondered about my dark hair and skin?"

"Not really," Naomi said, somewhat shocked.

"That's not what your blinking eyes say," Susan said. "He can track as good as a Shawnee too. We never fail to have deer or turkey when we have a taste for it."

Naomi wanted to know more about John's family tree, but didn't care to pry. "Maybe you should show Stephen how to track. I'd like having more game on the table." She stood, anxious to get home. "Let me see how my family got along without me."

Done with her goodbyes, Naomi climbed aboard the wagon and waved at the family in the doorway, and Rufus's big hooves clomped down the road. Nearing the place where Red broke his leg, she expected to see buzzards soaring in the sky, brilliantly blue, but saw none. Perhaps it was too cold for even them to take flight. No doubt they would as the day warmed.

Within a mile, the sun warmed her black bonnet and cloak, but not past comfort. Chains alongside the wagon rattled. The cold air chilled her nose, adding its note of freshness.

Around the final curve, when the cabin came into view, she realized the sun was higher in the sky than she thought it should be. Perhaps she had spent more time talking with Naomi while John used Rufus to move Red than it seemed. Not only had she been away from home overnight, she had been away over twenty-four hours, likely closer to thirty.

She stopped Rufus at the front door.

Stephen came out smiling; then his smile fell. "Where's Timmy and Lucy?"

About to climb down from the wagon, Naomi stopped. "What do you mean? They're supposed to be here."

"They left a note yesterday saying they were going to see you."

"I don't understand. Why would they leave a note when you were here?"

"I went after some turkeys in the Wilderness and it took a while."

Tempted to jump from the wagon, Naomi didn't because her knees would give out. "Are you saying they've been missing since I left yesterday morning?"

Stephen's face paled. "I … I don't …"

Willing strength into her legs, Naomi jumped from the wagon. She wanted to cry, to scream, to fall to her knees and pray, but only actions would locate her precious children. "Could they have followed you into the Wilderness and gotten lost?"

Like a fish out of water, Stephen worked

his mouth opened and closed, opened and closed. Naomi pushed by him and went inside. "Thank *Gott* Lucy has her cloak and Timmy has his coat. "What do we do, Stephen?" she wailed. "We've got to find them."

Stephen took the musket from over the fireplace. "I'll find them. Stay here."

"Go ahead but don't stay long. I'll get John. He said his grandfather taught him to track."

Stephen fetched powder and shot, donned his coat and wide-brimmed hat, and shoved through the door.

In tears, Naomi climbed into the wagon and snapped the reins against Rufus's broad back. *Dear Gott, Father in Heaven, please watch over Lucy and Timmy. Keep them safe from all harm and —*

Several unbidden thoughts brought more tears.

What if all the Shawnee haven't gone west?

What about bears, wolves, and cougars? How cold did it get last night? What if—Gott forbid—the rumors about Black Ears are true, and he's still in the Wilderness, waiting for his next victims?

Chapter 7

Holding the musket at the ready, Stephen stepped over dead trees, crossed creeks, climbed hills, and entered bottoms. Each step released the aroma of crunching leaves, similar to the herbal smell of cured tobacco. A constant prayer of safety for his children ran through his mind. Although his heart thudded in his temples from the effort of his search, it also thudded from the fear of what he might find—two young bodies, cold and stiff from death, possibly eaten by some creature.

He checked the position of the sun and turned back. However John knew the skill of tracking, it should come in handy, even if it meant returning home with two bodies.

As he left the woods, the jangle of the wagon made him look across the field. Instead of Naomi driving the wagon, John drove it, which made sense. If the two husbands were bound for a lengthy search, the two wives would be better off with each other's company. Stephen would make sure to tell them if it seemed the search would take longer than a day.

John jumped from the wagon and ran across the field until he reached Stephen. "Did you see any sign of them?"

"Not a trace."

"Naomi said they might've followed you into the woods. Since they left a note, let's check the road to my house for tracks first."

They returned to the wagon. Stephen climbed in and took the reins. John stayed on the ground. "I'll stay ahead and watch the road. I'll hold up my hand if I see anything."

Stephen followed John, whose head was

down, no doubt with his eyes focused on the dirt road. He strode quickly, sometimes moving to the side of the road. Stephen wanted to ask how he knew the skill of tracking, but finding his children was important, not small talk.

Nearing the fork in the road, John raised his hand and faced Stephen. "Is it possible they took the wrong fork? It's been a while since they visited Susan and me."

"I suppose. Let's take a look." Stephen knew the road into the Wilderness was less traveled than the road to town, so any tracks might show better.

Almost as soon as John took the fork, he raised his hand. Then he squatted. "I see prints like the hard heels of the shoes we wear." He stood and continued, and Stephen urged Rufus forward.

Maybe a half mile further, John stopped at the side of the road and knelt again. This time his forehead creased with worry. "I was afraid of this."

Fear shot through Stephen's heart. He jumped from the wagon. "What is it?"

John pointed to a foot print. "This came from a wolf." He looked up the road. "It ran that way." He followed the track and stopped again. "Here's two sets of children's shoe tracks going into the woods. The wolf was chasing them."

Stephen tied Rufus's reins to a bush and followed John into the woods. *Dear Gott, please, please, please let my children be safe. If something happened to them, I'm not sure Naomi and I will want to go on without them.* Along with the fear of losing his children, the disappointment at his lack of faith shuddered his shoulders.

John stopped to study some disturbed leaves, then continued, stopping as a flock of buzzards left the ground ahead in a dark cloud of flapping wings.

A knot the size of a hen's egg lodged in Stephen's throat; his prayers refused to move it.

John hurried to what was left of a furred creature on the ground. He pointed. "That looks like an arrow wound in its chest." He stepped to a tree near the wolf and studied the bark, reached up to a limb and pinched something from it. "This is a tiny piece of leather from a shoe sole. I think Timmy and Lucy climbed this tree to get away from the wolf, and an Indian killed it."

"That makes no sense," Stephen said. "If the Indian was friendly, he could've helped the children get home."

John's jaw clenched. "What if the Indian is Black Ears?"

"I thought he was just a rumor."

"Unfortunately, Rumors have their basis in fact. I also heard some people in town say he didn't leave with his tribe." John took a few steps away from the tree and knelt by a clump of overturned leaves. "He was on horseback." He raised his head and looked ahead. "The leaves look like more than one person walked deeper into the Wilderness." He turned to face Stephen. "I'm afraid he's taken Lucy and Timmy."

Stephen's legs buckled; he dropped to his knees. "Oh, *Gott* … oh, *Gott*. What will I tell Naomi?"

John knelt before him. "I know this is a terrible thing, but we must focus on the problem at hand. First, if we track them, what are you willing to do to get them back?" He pressed his palm to Stephen's shoulder. "Our *Ordnung* forbids violence, but this situation will likely call for violence. If it comes to getting your children back, can you shoot Black Ears?"

The name sent a surge of anger into Stephen's heart. Then his anger faded with *Gott's* words in the Bible: *Thou shalt not kill.* But what about a situation like this? Was he expected to simply let Black Ears, a man whose rumored past included violence and death, kill Timmy and Lucy? A picture formed in Stephen's mind he couldn't ignore: the children lying dead, their ears, smoked black over a fire, strung with those of numerous other victims. *Gott, please forgive me, but I cannot let my children meet such a fate.*

John squeezed Stephen's shoulder. "It's a difficult decision, but I couldn't stand by and do nothing if Susan and our new son were taken by a savage such as Black Ears."

Stephen raised his eyes to his friend. "I'll do what I must, even if Bishop Miller wants to shun me."

"We can ask forgiveness. I understand *Gott's* word, but evil must be fought. Good people shouldn't be forced to live in fear of death and suffering, and the only way they can do that is to fight back."

Standing, Stephen nodded. "I wish that weren't the case. Do you want to go on, or should we tell Naomi and Susan?"

"Let's go on. Since Black Ears is taking the

children deeper into the Wilderness, we might catch him in his camp."

Stephen noticed lines of worry around John's eyes. "What is it?"

"I'm afraid we might not catch him. Knowing the rumors about him, he often kidnapped Iroquois children and sold them to other tribe members. Since the Shawnee have gone west, he might've left to find someone to sell Timmy and Lucy to." John's chest rose and fell with a heavy breath. "Let's find his camp if we can. Then we can decide what to do."

Dread compressed Stephen's heart. Again he prayed for his children's safety, this time adding to be forgiven if he killed Black Ears.

Behind him, as he followed John, the wingbeats of the buzzards settling to feed deepened his dread. What would they find in Black Ears' camp? Would they find too small bodies, their ears taken? Would they find nothing? If so, would there be any clues as to the direction they had gone?

Through the budding tree limbs overhead, the sun pierced their skeletal fingers. The day warmed. Sweat dampened the hair below Stephen's wide-brimmed hat. After about a half mile, it trickled from his underarms and down his sides. A deer crossed in front of them, then another and another. Thank *Gott* they hadn't seen any bears or cougars, for their muskets might not stop them.

John stopped and nodded his head forward. "See those embers smoking? Black Ears is getting careless in his old age."

Muskets ready, they entered the camp. A frame of sticks for a hide tent was left, but little else.

John pointed to some disturbed leaves. "They're heading west, in a hurry. Let's run along that path until we can verify it. Then we need to buy horses and provisions in town."

"Why can't we take the wagon?" Stephen asked. "We can't waste time buying things."

John swallowed, evidenced by the muscles in his neck tightening. "The children were taken yesterday morning. That means Black Ears has a full day's start. This is going to be a long search. We might find him and the children in a day, but it might take longer. We need to be prepared regardless." He paused. "We also need to tell Susan and Naomi. Bishop Miller and the sheriff should know too."

Stephen didn't like his friend's statement, but it made sense. "Let's buy a pistol and a hunting knife each, and plenty of powder and shot. I want to be ready for anything."

Feeling as if he were going off to war, he followed John back to Rufus and the wagon, circling around the feeding buzzards. They climbed aboard. Within minutes, they hopped out of the wagon at John's house, where Naomi ran out to meet them. In tears, no doubt because Timmy and Lucy weren't with them, she fell into Stephen's arms. "Please," she sobbed. "Don't tell me they're … they're …"

Stephen steeled himself. Although the children weren't—that he knew of—dead, being taken by Black Ears was the next worst thing. He gripped Naomi's arms and looked into her eyes. "Have faith. They aren't dead, but they've been taken by Black Ears. John and I are going to buy horses in town. We'll track him and get them back."

"But what if … what if you have to kill him? It goes against everything we Amish stand for."

Wanting to be positive, though the scenario wasn't likely, Stephen continued. "We'll do the best we can, but if we must choose between violence and saving the children, we'll save the children."

"But you'll be shunned."

"Not if we ask forgiveness."

"It's not the same. You know you're

going to break our rules before you break them, so you might not be forgiven."

A Bible verse came to Stephen's mind: *Isaiah 41:10 - Fear thou not; for I am with thee: be not dismayed; for I am thy Gott: I will strengthen thee; yea, I will help thee; yea, I will uphold thee with the right hand of my righteousness.*

"We do our best to be righteous people," he told his wife. "*Gott* will be with us with his right hand of righteousness. Even if we must kill to save Timmy and Lucy, *Gott* will forgive us though our brethren shun us. I pray that doesn't happen, but if I do nothing, I can never forgive myself—not only for not saving Timmy and Lucy, but for not preventing Black Ears from harming anyone else. Evil cannot be allowed to grow. The men of the Bible fought evil, so we must fight evil as well."

John came from his house with two leather packs. "I've got water and food and shot and powder. We'll shoot game if we're out more than a few days."

Susan came from the house, a bundle in her arms. "I'll pray for you and your family," she told Stephen.

John climbed into the wagon. "Let's tell Bishop Miller and get to town. I want to start right after."

Naomi told them to wait. She ran inside and came back wearing her black cloak and bonnet. "I'll take you to town and bring Rufus and the wagon back. Then I can tend the cow and the chickens at home."

Minutes later, Rufus's hooves were clomping along the dirt road. Sitting beside his wife, Stephen admired her. Once the task had been set, she strived to meet it. *Gott* had surely blessed him with a fine woman.

A few miles later, at Bishop Miller's cabin, he came out of his home to the jangle of the wagon's chains and waved. "Well, well, is this an early Easter visit?"

Stephen climbed from the wagon,

followed by John. "I wish it were an Easter visit," John said.

Stephen explained everything. By the time he said they were going to track Black Ears to rescue Timmy and Lucy, Bishop Miller's lips had tightened into a thin line. "You won't be able to rescue them without a fight. If you resort to violence, you'll be breaking your vows.

Anger flooded Stephen's face with heat. "If we resort to violence, you'll shun us."

"Violence isn't our way," the bishop said, his voice stern.

"Am I just supposed to let Timmy and Lucy be killed, or worse? Could you do that if they were your children?"

"I would trust *Gott*. Even if they died, they would go to Heaven."

John glanced at Stephen, then faced the bishop. "We mean no disrespect to our *Ordnung,* but when we allow evil to flourish, what good is being good? Eventually the world will be filled with evil then. Wars were fought in the Bible, and you're saying we can't even rescue two children from a terrible fate?"

The bishop's eyes softened. "If you must go, remember to pray. Do so for every minute you're awake. *Gott* will answer you. I'm sure of it." He bowed his head. "Dear Lord, please be with Timmy and Lucy. Give them strength instead of fear. Give them peace instead of anxiety. Have them pray for the man who has taken them, so Your word will enter his heart and change it. Send this prayer to them—John 11:25-26. 'Jesus said to her, I am the resurrection and the life. The one who believes in me will live, even though they die; and whoever lives by believing in me will never die.' Amen.'" The bishop opened his eyes. "I'll gather everyone together to pray for your children, Stephen." He looked up at Naomi in the wagon seat. "Have faith, dear sister. Miracles still happen."

"And what if the man's heart doesn't change?" Stephen asked. "Will *Gott* strike him down for me?"

John clasped Stephen's shoulder. "Hurting anyone is the last thing we want." He faced the bishop. "We'll try out best not to do so. Thank you for having everyone pray."

After their goodbyes, Naomi snapped the reins, Stephen beside her and John in back. Except for the jangle of the chains, the rattle of the wagon wheels when they hit a rut, and the occasional snort from Rufus, the ride to town was silent.

It being a Saturday, the dirt street was busy with people. Stephen kept his eyes ahead to avoid the stares, praying for *Gott* to touch their hearts to draw them closer to Him. Life is too short to think material things are the way to happiness. Only gratitude for *Gott's* blessings—the rain, the good earth, tilling the ground for one's food, and the love found in a caring family and with good friends—can accomplish that.

Nearing the sheriff's office and jail, Naomi pulled the reins, stopping Rufus. She faced Stephen, tears running down her cheeks. He raised his palm to her face, surrounded by the black bonnet. "I love you, Naomi. I'll do my best to follow our *Ordnung,* but I make no promises about sparing a man's life who is bent on harming our children."

She pressed her hand to his. "I trust you, my husband, but I trust *Gott* too. With everyone praying, I know you'll bring Timmy and Lucy home."

Stephen noticed she didn't say he would bring them home safe. No doubt she meant that, but the thought of what Black Ears might do to them—might've already done to them—broke his heart. "Pray as hard as you can, my dear wife. I don't want to harm anyone, but I can't stand the thought of losing our precious children. They're gifts from *Gott,* so why would he bless us with them, only to take them from us?"

Naomi blinked; a single tear tracked down her cheek. "All we can do is have faith. Do you want me to stay until you and John get horses and talk to the sheriff?"

Stephen glanced at the livery stable. "You can go home. Will you stay there or stay with Susan?"

"Except for taking care of the chickens and the cow, I'll stay with her. We'll bring each other comfort."

John climbed from the wagon. Stephen kissed his dear wife's forehead and joined him. After a single wave, she snapped the reins and steered Rufus out of town.

Doubts filled Stephen's mind as her black cloak and bonnet grew smaller in the distance—doubts of even himself returning, much less the children.

Shaking his head, he followed John to the sheriff's office. Beneath the porch, Allen Poor, the metal star on his chest tarnished, looked up. "What can I do for you gentlemen today?"

"What's the chance you could help us with a kidnapping?" John asked. "Stephen's children were taken by Black Ears."

Sheriff Poor's bushy eyebrows rose. "I 'spose that's why you're armed. I thought you people didn't believe in violence."

"We don't," Stephen said to the man who gambled and visited the bawdy house.

"Then why are you armed?"

"Insurance," John said.

"Them smoothbore muskets ain't much insurance. Best get two rifled-barrel ones. Then you can take out Black Ears at 200 yards instead of 100. Make sure to get two with light triggers. Makes you more accurate." He spat tobacco juice to the wooden porch's floor. "I wish you well, but not with me going. I gotta tend the hoodlums in our fair town."

Stephen expected as much. He left for the

general store, where he and John traded their muskets for two new rifles with the lightest triggers they could find, not worrying with the pistols. Moments later they saddled two horses and were galloping back to the Wilderness to pick up the trail.

Chapter 8

The farther away from the Wilderness Black Ears went, the more he considered killing his captives and continuing west to be with his people. If he did, he could speak with the chief, a much younger man than him, who he appointed when they left, about where they planned to settle. He also wanted to speak with their shaman about the spirit world. Since his children were dead, he wanted to know if he would see them and his wife again after his death. He longed for this more than any other thing in his life, even more than killing settlers.

Setting those thoughts aside, he sat up

straight to stretch his aching back from the long ride. He and his captives had ridden all day, and they were now a two day journey from the Wilderness. If anyone were coming for them, they would've arrived by now. Regardless, he would keep up the pace.

Toward dusk, when it was time to make camp, they approached the bank of a river. Unlike most Shawnee, Black Ears feared rivers. He had heard one too many stories of a warrior attacked by poisonous water snakes. Just the thought of a snake sinking its fangs in his flesh made the skin on his back quiver like when a horse quivered its skin to make flies buzz away. Still, he wanted to cross the river before dark instead of waiting. This side had few trees. The other side had more, some with dead limbs for making a fire with little smoke.

Black Ears looked at the children behind him. "Hold tight to the saddle. If you fall off, you fall off."

The girl's mouth fell open. "You mean you'll let us drown?"

Saying nothing, Black Ears eased the horse down the bank and into the river. Beside him, the girl clucked her tongue, and her horse did the same. The horse's legs swished water. His knickered. The other one stopped to drink. Before Black Ears could stop his horse, the rope tightened and jerked his horse, startling it. It eared and snorted. Water flew, wetting Black Ears, and he imagined dozens of squirming snakes beneath the water, waiting to bite him.

The horse reared higher; its head jerked up and down, snatching the reins from Black Ears' hands. He tumbled backward off the horse, trying not to scream as he went under the water. All around him, a coiled mass of snakes uncoiled to squirm into his clothes, around his neck, up his pants legs, up his sleeves, into his ears, his nostrils, his eyes, his mouth. One of the snakes resembled a rope. He grabbed it and pulled himself to shallower water and stood.

Holding the other end of the rope, the boy tilted his head to one side. "That was funny. I never heard a person scream under water."

The girl's eye brightened as if she wanted to laugh. If she did, Black Ears would cut her throat. He looked down at the water. A dark area showed he had fallen into a hole, and not a single snake was there. His cheeks heated with embarrassment at such a stupid thing.

Standing in the knee-deep water, his hair dripping, his buckskins soaked, his pride injured, Black Ears fingered the handle of the knife at his belt as his enemies waited for him to do something. He waved at the far bank. "We're camping there. Go gather firewood."

The boy jerked the rope. "We can't go

anywhere until you do. The rope is tied to your horse."

Again, Black Ears fingered the knife's handle. Their throats would slice like butter beneath the blade. Not yet. Not yet.

Astride his horse, he led them to the bank. They gathered wood. Two arrows made short work of two squirrels. Soon, as the eastern horizon darkened, they were roasting over the fire, skewered on green sticks.

In the woods behind them, a lone cricket chirped. The night air grew cool. The children sat closer to the fire. The girl wrapped her arms around her black cloak. The boy stuck his hands in his coat pockets. Beneath the boy's wide-brimmed hat and the girl's black bonnet, the fire bathed their faces with flickering light. Above the budding tree limbs, an endless display of stars dotted the sky.

Black Ears turned the squirrels.

Seasons ago, when he was a young man with a young wife, he loved sitting by the fire on nights like this. Their son and daughter, instead of asking where the stars came from like most children, simply stared at them in wonder. How innocent they were, enjoying the natural world in all of its beauty.

Releasing the memory before it burned his eyes with tears, he studied his captives. Like his own children, their faces were turned toward the sky, but their eyes were closed and their lips were moving.

"What are you doing?" he asked.

The girl raised her palm toward him as if she demanded he not bother them. He fingered the knife's handle, tempted to use the blade now.

She lowered her head and opened her eyes, followed by the boy doing the same. "We were praying," he said.

"We heard the Shawnee pray," the girl said. "We pray to *Gott*. Who do you pray to?"

"Your *Gott* is weak, or you wouldn't be here with me. I pray to Mishe Moneto. In your language, Mishe Moneto is Great Spirit."

"What's great about him?" the boy asked. "Does he forgive your sins?"

Black Ears blew a disgusted breath. "Forgive? Warriors need no such thing."

The girl glanced at the boy. "Don't you know the difference between right and wrong?" she asked Black Ears.

He waved the silly question away. "What I know —"

"He doesn't know," the boy interrupted. "He might if someone took his children like he took us. It would make him sad like we know it's making *Daat* and *Maam* sad."

"I miss them," the girl whispered, looking at her hands in her lap. She raised her head to study Black Ears. "Did you have children?"

Instead of answering, he drew the knife and sliced meat from one of the squirrels. Satisfied it was done, he cut it in half and tossed the pieces to his captives. "Eat and sleep."

The boy gnawed at his piece of squirrel, chewed and swallowed. "You're old. Do you have grandchildren? Is your wife still alive?"

Black Ears peered into the boy's blue eyes. "You ask too many questions."

"You don't answer them."

Standing, Black Ears turned as if leaving the fire and jumped over it to jerk the boy up by the collar. He drew the knife and pressed the blade to his throat. "You will stop asking questions if I cut your tongue out."

"Please," the girl begged, "he won't ask any more questions."

Black Ears dropped the boy to the ground and returned to his seat to eat the squirrel. The children did the same.

111

The night air grew even colder. He added wood to the fire, tied his captives, and lay down wrapped in the deer skins.

The boy lay close to the fire. The girl lay behind him, draping the cloak over them both. With each breath, a white cloud puffed from her nostrils. Because of the heat from the fire, no cloud puffed from the boy's nostrils.

Black Ears wondered if his children lay like this after the Iroquois captured them. Then he stopped wondering. If not, he would imagine theirs screams as they were tortured by the group who had bought them. In his anger and rage, he had killed the last warrior without making him admit where the children had died. He should've controlled himself better. Then he could've buried them properly.

The night drew on. The fire died to embers. Black Ears' back ached from his fall into the river. The few teeth he had left ached from chewing the tough squirrel.

The stars glinted. A Great Horned Owl silently glided to a limb on a nearby oak and turned its head around to study the old Shawnee and his two captives. Its eyes reflected the embers, reflected the scene, reflected this very moment amongst all the years Black Ears had lived. It seemed Mishe Moneto was trying to tell him something important, and because of the sign of the owl, the message was of death, and to kill the captives in revenge for his own children's deaths. The thought brought comfort. Black Ears lowered his face into the warmth of the dear hides and closed his eyes.

Chapter 9

Having risen early, Naomi took Rufus and the wagon home. She fed the chickens and the cow, gathered eggs and filled a pail with milk. At Susan's cabin again, she cracked eggs into the pan over the fireplace.

Her every waking moment was filled with prayer, and Susan said hers was two.

At home, Naomi had found the turkey in the ice house. How could she and Stephen consider Easter and eating with the children gone? She was tempted to throw it outside for the buzzards. After all, if not for Stephen going after a turkey, the children wouldn't have left without him knowing it, and he might've come with them here.

Feeding the baby in bed, Susan stopped to pat the tiny back. "I'll be up soon to help."

"You need to rest," Naomi said, scrambling the eggs. "Besides, I like to stay busy, so I'll tend to your cow and chickens after we eat." She didn't say the rest: *And so I won't think how of Lucy and Timmy are suffering at the hands of Black Ears.* Although she understood the bishop's words about not harming anyone, Amish women weren't supposed to question the men concerning their *Ordnung.* What would he think of Luke 22-36, where Jesus told his disciples to buy swords? Surely they didn't need swords for anything but defending themselves, like Stephen wanted to defend Lucy and Timmy. Were good people just supposed to let evil people rob and kill them? Jesus's word in the Bible said no, as well as Gott's statement on defending one's self from thieves in the night, with death if necessary.

115

Susan placed the baby in the crib and dressed, started a pot of coffee and sat at the table. "You're right about me needing to rest. I'm still sore too."

"You'll get over it soon," Naomi said, plating the eggs.

When the aroma of coffee steamed from the pot, Susan filled cups and warmed some leftover biscuits. Her silence concerning Timmy and Susan said a thousand things, none of them comforting. Breakfast kept the same silent theme. So did washing and drying dishes, but Naomi noticed her friend's lips moving with solemn prayer.

As she put the last dish away, a horse snorted outside. At the window by the cabin door, Susan faced Naomi. "It's Bishop Miller." Before he could knock, Susan welcomed him in. *"Gude mariye,* Bishop."

He removed his wide-brimmed hat. "It would be a much better morning if all your family members were here. Our community is praying as hard as they can, but I thought we could gather tonight and do so. We can sing and praise *Gott* and join our voices in prayer for the safe return of Timmy and Lucy." He looked away and back. "Without violence, of course."

Naomi's cheeks flared with heat. "I'd prefer they return, however it happens." She wanted to add the verses in the Bible about self-defense, but knew she shouldn't to avoid an argument.

"I have a question," Susan said.

"What about?" the bishop said.

"In the Bible, *Gott* says a thief can be killed. Then why can't a murderer like Black Ears be killed?"

"Well ..." The bishop's lips twisted side to side. "The Bible says a thief can only be killed at night."

Susan slapped her hands to her hips. "So a thief can be killed to protect property while a murderer can't be killed to protect precious children." She faced Naomi. "That

117

makes as much sense as a rooster laying eggs."

"Know your place, ladies," the bishop said.

Naomi chewed her lip. "My place as a mother is to care for my children." She hesitated. Speak her mind about Jesus telling the disciples to buy swords or not? Stephen would say not, but he wasn't here.

She met the bishop's stare. "In Luke 22-36, Jesus told his disciples to buy swords. They didn't need swords for anything but defending themselves, like Stephen wants to defend Lucy and Timmy. How do you explain that?"

The bishop covered his mouth, as if he were a man who didn't think women should be reading the Bible. "As I told you both, women should know their place concerning our doctrine."

"Let's hope your daughters aren't taken by some savage," Naomi blurted. "Then you'd see how it feels."

"Feelings are the problem," the bishop asserted. "That's why women can't discuss Biblical doctrine logically."

"Women with perspective can," Susan said. "I agree, some women see things one way, but men do that too. It takes a person who can see both sides of an issue to make decisions. No person is right all the time. That's why we use the Bible to guide our way. *Gott* understands all sides of an issue instead of just one, like with loving us despite our sins."

Well said, Naomi thought. "I apologize for us approaching you like this, Bishop Miller. All we want is for our loved ones to return. Surely you can understand that."

"Which is why I came to tell you about our gathering tonight," the bishop mumbled, clearly bothered by his authority being challenged.

I just had a baby," Susan said. "I want to come but I can't."

"I'll be there," Naomi said. "What time?"

The bishop told her seven and bid them good day. Pressing his hat to his head, he closed the door behind him.

"Well," Susan said to Naomi, "that went well." She covered a giggle. "Were we too hard on him?"

Naomi grinned. "Not too bad. We should have the right to question doctrine like anyone else. After all, the answers came straight from the Bible."

Susan patted Naomi's arm. "It's good to see you smile. *Gott* will bring your family home safely. I'm sure of it."

In his crib, the baby—Naomi knew it was time to think of him as John Jr.,—started to cry. "I think someone's ready to eat again."

Susan took him from the crib and sat in a rocker by the fireplace to feed him, which filled Naomi with love for her own family. She prayed for them—prayed for Lucy and Timmy's safety, prayed for Stephen and

John and the decision they would have to make upon getting Black Ears in their musket sights, prayed violence could be avoided if at all possible.

She poured more coffee for herself and went to the window, wondering if Stephen and John were safe in their travels.

* * *

Done with a hot cup of coffee to ward off the morning chill, Stephen rinsed it with water and returned it to his pack. Across the fire, John rinsed the dregs from the pot and packed it away.

Astride the horses, they continued on Black Ears' trail. John had lost it twice, from when it had gone into a creek and come out a mile away. Either the old Shawnee thought someone was following him, or he was being cautious. If only they knew.

The second time they had lost the trail, they happened on a farmer who said he saw an Indian and two children on horseback. Before thanking him and picking up the trail, Stephen faced the man. "Didn't you think it was odd for two Amish children to be with an Indian?"

"None of my business," the farmer grumbled.

"That Indian took my children," Stephen explained, ashamed of the rage burning in his heart. "If they were *your* children, I'm sure they would be your business. When good people just stand and watch as someone harms others, evil grows like a cancer, until it consumes everything."

The farmer frowned. "Shoulda known you was one of them Bible thumpers. Oughta shoot the whole lot of 'em, trying to shove religion down folk's throats."

"Sir," John said, "*Gott's* word is free for the taking, the same as His forgiveness. Whether you accept or not is your choice. Thank you for helping us. We'll be on our way."

Regardless of Stephen's anger, he

touched the brim of his hat, thanked the farmer, and followed John.

As the horses trotted along, with John eyeing the ground, Stephen prayed to *Gott* to help them avoid violence. At the same time, though, he thought of any future victims of Black Ears if they didn't kill him. How many more men would die by his arrows? How many more women would be violated? How many more children would be taken to suffer? Yes, violence was wrong, but allowing savages such as Black Ears to harm others—plus harming more people in the future—was worse.

John's horse moved closer. "The more I think about it, the more I hope we don't have to kill Black Ears."

"I disagree," Stephen said, avoiding the urge to not narrow his eyes at his friend. "Think of the people who would still be alive if someone had killed him long ago. Then think of all the people we might save besides Timmy and Lucy. How people can

123

ignore that makes no sense. When good folks can't be safe and work and love their families because of people like Black Ears, we have no rights at all. If that's the case, why did Washington and Jefferson and all the founders fight to create this country?" Stephen shook his head bitterly. "Just to let people with no regard for others ruin it?" He patted the rifle in its scabbard hanging from the saddle. "If I get Black Ears in my sights, not only will I save Timmy and Lucy, I'll save countless others from the same fate."

John looked away and back: a man weighing his words. "That makes sense, I suppose. Imagine our country in the future. It'll be filled with millions of people, and many of those people will be like Black Ears. If sheriffs and judges don't put them in jail where they belong, evil will ruin the country."

Stephen nodded. "Then we know what

we need to do."

No rain had fallen recently. Dust puffed up from the horse's hooves on the narrow road through the woods, but at least it made for easy tracking. About a quarter mile ahead, the woods opened into a field of tall grass atop rolling hills with a stream running through it, the perfect place to graze and water the horses. As if sensing what Stephen was thinking, or either they smelled the water and the lush grass, the horses knickered. Then, nostrils flaring, they broke into a gallop straight for the field and the stream.

"I don't blame them!" John yelled. "We haven't had fresh water for a while now!"

Not used to riding horses, Stephen could only hold the reins and keep his feet in the stirrups. Ahead of him, in one quick movement, John's horse stumbled and fell. Jerking the reins, Stephen slowed his horse and steered it back to his friend.

Wild-eyed in the grass, the horse kicked

and screamed, its front leg broken.

John stood, rubbing his wrist. "I can't believe it. Another groundhog hole got this horse like the one that got Red." He jerked his rifle from the scabbard and shot the squealing horse one handed, which worried Stephen.

"Is your arm broken?" he asked, waving away the bitter cloud of burnt gunpowder.

John flexed his left wrist and winced. "Or it's badly sprained. I'm sorry, but I can't go on. If you see Black Ears, you won't be able to run him down with me on your horse."

"Maybe there's a town on the trail where we can buy one."

"He's avoided the towns. Help me setup camp by the stream. I've taught you enough about tracking to find Timmy and Lucy. Come back for me when you rescue them."

At the stream, less than fifty paces away, Stephen built his friend a fire to make coffee. Then he went back for his belongings and the saddle. "What'll you eat? We don't have much food left."

John shared a wry grin. "That horse wasn't good for avoiding groundhog holes, but he'll be good for filling my stomach."

In turn, Stephen looked at his friend, the dead horse, and the position of the sun in the sky. Half a day of sunlight remained, so he should get going. "I hate to leave you, John."

John was reloading the rifle. "I'll be all right. Go ahead. I'll pray for you and your children."

Sighing deeply, Stephen heeled the horse's flanks and set off through the grass, where the tracks of the two horses he and John—now just him—were pursuing had left a trodden path.

Chapter 10

Astride his horse, Black Ears looked back at the boy and girl. In their black clothes, they resembled two unhappy crows, eyes down, faces dirty, hair falling from beneath the bonnet and the hat. He faced ahead.

Soon he would be singing war songs with his people. If none of them wanted the children, he would torture them himself. He knew many ways to cause pain, and he would smile as they screamed.

Last night, the girl cried for the first time, begging her god to save her and her brother. Sleeping next to the fire with her arm around him, he patted her hand on his chest and said not to cry, that it would be all right.

For the briefest moment, sorrow entered Black Ears' heart, until he rolled over to not see them. Maybe he was getting soft in his old age, or maybe he was thinking about his own children and how they met their ends when they were tortured.

The noon sun glared down from the sky. In the distance, across an expanse of weeds and brush, a group of buildings shimmered against the horizon. Black Ears shaded his eyes. A woman was hanging clothes on a line. A man was plowing behind a mule. Minutes later, as they rode closer, the scene grew clearer. The woman's belly was rounded with child, which gave Black Ears an idea for another torture.

From behind him, one of the children coughed. "I'm hungry and thirsty," the boy said. "You didn't give us anything this morning."

To be deprived of his captives from starvation would be a shame. Now noticing the distant white specks of chickens in front of one of the buildings, he heeled his horse's flanks.

As he approached the man and woman, they looked up and then looked at each other. The man joined the woman and waited, unaware of the fate they would meet.

Black Ears pointed at the chickens. "Cook two for us. I need to feed these children. I found them lost and I'm taking them home."

"The closest Amish are east," the man said. "You're going west."

Black Ears fingered the handle of his knife. "Where I am going is none of your business. Kill two chickens and have your woman cook them."

With an ax in a chopping block by one of the buildings, the man made short work of two chickens. The woman plucked them and went in the house. Black Ears motioned toward a well. "Draw water. We need to drink."

The man did so, setting the pail on the rock circle surrounding the well. Black Ears climbed off the horse and drank the cool, sweet water. He motioned to the children. They climbed down and did the same.

The hint of smoke from the house's chimney increased. Black Ears imagined the sizzle and aroma of chicken frying. After drinking more water, he faced the man. "Does your woman make bread?"

"She makes biscuits."

"Tell her to make some."

"We have some leftover from breakfast." The man's eyes darted to the ax in the chopping block.

"Why would you harm an old man trying to help two children?" Black Ears asked, wishing the man would try.

"I ... I was thinking about chopping some wood," the man said, his voice quavering.

Black Ears palmed water from the pail

and scrubbed his face. "You have enough wood. Go inside." He motioned to the children to follow him, and they all entered the house.

At a fireplace, the woman was turning the chicken in a black pan. Black Ears licked his lips at the browning skin. The children did too, amusing him. The man set a pan of the cold biscuits near the fire to warm. Then he filled three glasses with water from a pail and set them on a wooden table.

Black Ears noticed an empty gun rack over the fireplace mantle. "Where is your gun?"

"It's broken," the man said. "A neighbor's working on it for me."

The woman plated chicken and biscuits. The children sat, followed by Black Ears.

The woman, her yellow hair in a bun, waited by the fireplace, eyes steadily blinking, a hand on her belly. The man, his spine as straight as a tree, stood beside her.

Sweat beaded his brow. A brown beard colored his cheeks and chin. Every few minutes his Adam's apple bobbed, amusing Black Ears with his nervousness. Before he and the children left, his nervousness would change to terror when the blade of a knife opened his wife's belly.

The boy started to bite a biscuit and the girl elbowed him. His eyes widened with understanding of some kind. She removed her black bonnet and he removed his hat. With them beside their plates, they bowed their heads. "Dear *Gott*," the girl said, "please bless this food for the nourishment of our bodies. Bless the nice lady who cooked this chicken and made these biscuits, and bless the man who gave us water."

She paused. Black Ears fingered the handle of his knife. If she dared speak about him taking them. ...

"And please don't let *Maam* and *Daat* worry. I know you're watching out for us, and we'll be home soon." She paused again. "Bless those who have no love in their lives. Bless those who are old and angry. If they don't understand why, please enter their hearts and help them feel your love."

"And your forgiveness too," the boy chirped. "Like the time I put a frog down Lucy's collar, she was mad at first, but she forgave me when I 'pologized."

The girl giggled, amazing Black Ears with how she could do such a thing after being taken from her people to meet an unknown end.

"Please, *Gott*," the girl, Lucy, continued, "wipe all our tears away, and give us peace beyond all understanding, like when the sun rises in the morning and sets at night and the crickets chirp and when the Mourning Doves coo in the trees behind the cabin. Amen."

Her words made Black Ears work his jaw. How did this child know his favorite time of the day and his favorite things to hear? Was she a spirit of some kind, or maybe a shaman? Clenching his teeth, he scoffed at his thoughts and started to eat.

Lucy finished a chicken leg in just a few bites and looked over her shoulder at the woman. "Thank you, ma'am. This is delicious."

"It's my favorite," the boy said.

"What's your name, Son," the man asked.

"I'm, Timmy, sir. Nice to meet you."

Black Ears rolled his eyes at all the politeness. They'd be screaming soon enough, especially the woman. He jerked his knife from its sheath and drove it into the table. "Enough talk. Eat so I can get you home."

The man glanced at the woman. "For someone who claims to be doing a good deed, you sure don't act like it."

The woman shook her head: a person who wanted her husband to avoid bloodshed.

Grinning, Black Ears swallowed biscuit, finished another piece of chicken, and washed it down with the cool water. He looked down to pinch a morsel of meat from the plate, shoved it into his mouth, and looked up at the man and woman—and the man was pointing a musket at his chest. "I don't know who you are or what you're doing, but—"

Lucy jumped from her seat. "Please, sir. No one needs to get hurt."

A crisp click announced the man cocking the musket. "Young lady, since you're defending this man, I suppose he's taking you home like he says." He raised the rifle and sighted down the barrel. "But I don't have to like him for it."

Black Ears jerked the knife from the table. Instead of burying it in the man's chest, he slipped it into the sheath. He had stayed here too long anyway, letting his lust for revenge for his family's death get the best of him. "I appreciate the food," he said, every word boiling in his throat like bile.

The man motioned toward the door with the musket barrel. "Then be on your way."

Lucy and Timmy donned their headgear. "Thank you for everything," Timmy said, again chirping cheerily. "It was real fine."

Black Ears was tempted to backhand him. "Get out there and get on that horse so I can get you home."

Outside, he and his sister climbed into the saddle. Black Ears led both horses to a trough to drink, watching the man with the gun in the doorway, his finger on the trigger. He should've kept going. Not only had he let his lust for revenge ruin his judgment, he had let the time get away. The sun was sliding toward the horizon, and he wanted to camp in the next section of woods, a green area of trees miles away on the western horizon.

In the saddle, he heeled the horse into a gallop and hurried away from the man with the gun.

The miles passed. Weed and scrub brush gave way to sparse patches of grass and stunted trees. On one limb, an owl—a strange sight during the day—twisted its head to eye Black Ears. Despite the hot sunshine, a chill crawled down his spine. Death was coming for someone, and it might be him.

Inside the shade of the trees, the cool air dissipated his dread. After a few more miles, as the shade darkened to dusk, he made camp. Like his own children would do, Timmy and Lucy gathered wood without him demanding it.

A fire soon burned. He took his pack from the horse for water and frowned. The woman had gone outside once, saying she needed to relieve herself, and she had put the leftover chicken in the pack. Her generosity was a weakness. If not for the man with the gun, she would be dead.

The shadows lengthened. Through the tree limbs, a fingernail moon offered dim light. Mice rustled in the leaves. The air cooled. In the fire, a knot exploded, making him jump.

They finished the chicken and drank water. Curiosity drew Black Ear's eyes to the boy and girl—Timmy and Lucy. "Why do your people dress the same? I've seen you gather at different homes from time to time. When the wind blows your clothes, you look like a flock of crows flapping your wings."

The fire reflected in Lucy's eyes. "We're Amish. We're plain people. We dress the same to avoid pride."

"And to be different from other people," Timmy added.

Black Ears snorted laughter. "So you think you're better than everyone else."

"Not at all," Lucy said. "We're humble and don't care to stand apart from each other. We help each other in our community. The men can build a barn in a day."

Black Ears didn't laugh at that. His people worked together too. "What do your people do when you gather at different homes."

"Have you ever heard of church?" Timmy asked. "It's like that. We meet to pray and sing and listen to the bishop tell us lessons from the Bible."

"What is that?" Black Ears asked, curious about a word he didn't know.

"It's a book," Lucy said. "It's filled with the word of *Gott* about how to live and love each other and to work together."

"It's got lots of verses and stuff," Timmy said. He raised his hand and touched a finger. "It's got psalms" —he touched another finger— "and proverbs" he touched another finger— "and revelations. It's got test'ments too."

Lucy raised an eyebrow at him. "Testaments, not test'ments."

Timmy shook his head. "She likes to tell me what to do. Did your children do that to each other?"

About to chuckle at the boy, Black Ears recalled the memory of his children sitting by a fire exactly like this, teasing each other about something he'd forgotten, his wife smiling along with him as they listened. Then a thing that hadn't happened in years happened: he felt the burn of tears behind his eyes.

He lay down in the deerskins. "Go to sleep."

Timmy lay in his customary place by the fire, tugging his coat around him. "Why did you take us? We never did anything to you."

Lucy lay behind him, her arm around his waist. "You didn't answer about your children."

"Or why you took us," Timmy added a second time.

Scowling because he had forgotten to tie

them, Black Ears got up and did so. "No more talk. Go to sleep before I lose my patience."

They closed their eyes, yet their lips moved, likely in prayer like at the house of the man and the woman who had fed them.

Again he lay down. Again he wrapped the deerskins around him. Again the memories of his wife and children came to him. Again his eyes burned with tears.

He despised his weakness, brought on by these children. One day—likely one day soon—if they continued to make him feel this way, they would meet their end with the blade of his knife across their throats as they slept.

Chapter 11

Naomi donned her cloak and bonnet and faced Susan. "Well, I hope I don't get shunned tonight."

"You won't if our plan goes well." Susan kissed John Jr's. forehead as he slept in her arms, having just finished his supper by the fireplace while the rocking chair creaked.

A blustery wind had blown all day, so Naomi tied the bonnet securely. "Our community's opinion on the subject of defending ourselves matters. After all, both the New and Old Testaments say it's reasonable."

"Praise *Gott* for his word," Susan said. "I look forward to hearing what happens."

On the hard wagon seat, Naomi snapped

the reins. "Get up there, Rufus. This Amish woman is looking forward to this prayer meeting. My family's safety, and the safety of our community in this evil world, is counting on it."

A short time later, she tied Rufus's reins to one of several posts outside of Bishop Miller's home, where at least twenty wagons and buggies were also tied.

Inside the large cabin, when the door creaked open, the bearded faces of married men faced her, plus the shaven faces of unmarried men, all on one side of the room. On the other side, all the women wore white *kapps*, and each of them faced her too. Apparently she was the last person to arrive. She hung her cloak and bonnet on a rack by the door. Her shoes tapped the pine floor as she found a seat on a pew near the middle with the women.

"Please join me," Bishop Miller said from the other side of the room. Naomi did so.

Although she would usually lower her head meekly while facing everyone, this time she didn't. "Thank you all for coming. It's a terrible thing to bear, my family out in the world, possibly dead or dying at the hands of a savage."

Bishop Miller cleared his throat. "That savage is one of *Gott's* children. We must pray for his salvation."

On the men's side of the room, Caleb Schrock, Naomi's brother, stood, and her and Susan's plan took shape.

"We all pray he will seek salvation, Bishop. In the meantime, how do we prevent such a thing from happening again?"

"We don't," the bishop said sternly. *"Gott's* will takes many forms."

"What about the will of Satan? The Bible says he exists and influences people. Are we to simply let those people harm us at will?"

"If *Gott* allows Satan to influence people, He does it for a purpose."

Caleb hesitated, and Naomi knew why: what the bishop was saying made sense. Deciding she'd rather be sitting, she took a seat on the front pew.

Caleb cleared his throat. "*Gott* also allows us to kill game for the table. I know men are not game to be slaughtered, but the Bible says we can defend ourselves from thieves, and if we kill one, we aren't at fault."

Heads turned. People murmured. An elderly man with a gray beard to his chest stood. "Being a deacon, I've often considered these problems. The New Testament tells us that Jesus admonished His disciples to trade their garments for swords. He didn't do so for them to take game. He did so for defense."

More heads turned. More people murmured. Above Bishop Miller's beard, his cheeks reddened as if he didn't care to have his authority questioned. Looking down, he covered his mouth. "This is what

I get for allowing my congregation to read the Bible," he mumbled.

Caleb's wife, Fannie, stood. "I agree with *Gott* and Jesus. We should be able to defend ourselves if need be. If we do, isn't it *Gott's* will also? If not, we wouldn't be able to aim a gun or raise a knife to protect ourselves or a loved one."

Naomi didn't like the change of mood in the congregation, gone from solemn to disrespectful. She stood. "We've always voted on changes to our *Ordnung,* but I prefer to do so after my" —tears flooded her eyes— "if my family and John comes home. They deserve a vote as well. Right now we should pray for exactly that, preferably without harm to anyone."

Everyone sat. The congregation quieted. She sat and faced the bishop. "Please lead us in prayer, Bishop Miller."

He bowed his head. "'Rejoice always, pray without ceasing, give thanks in all circumstances; for this is the will of *Gott* in

Christ Jesus for you.'"

The congregation joined in: "'Rejoice always, pray without ceasing, give thanks in all circumstances; for this is the will of *Gott* in Christ Jesus for you.'"

On and on the prayer continued, with the bishop adding similar verses. Naomi waited, hoping to have her feeling of hopelessness replaced by the feeling of hope. Instead, dread sank its weight upon her shoulders. Perhaps it was the mix of voices. Perhaps it was the mix of sincerity and hopelessness. Perhaps it was—*Gott* forbid—a lack of her own faith, brought on by what could happen to her precious family. Regardless, to give herself a setting for the most earnest prayer she could manage, she would spend the night at home, elbows on the table, hands clasped, an oil lamp pooling its light around her, and plead with every ounce of strength she possessed for *Gott* to bring her family home.

Chapter 12

Done with a quick breakfast in the saddle, Stephen heeled the horse's flanks.

The last two days, he had managed with four hours of sleep each night, staying on the trail to gain miles on his children. Thank *Gott*, no rain had ruined the tracks of the two horses, whether in dirt, forest paths, or in fields of grass and brush. Also, the tracks seemed fresher now, with crisper instead of crumbling edges.

Nodding off, he tried to keep the horse at a steady trot, but every time his eyes closed, the horse seemed to sense it and slowed to a slow walk. Then the smell of woodsmoke snapped his eyes fully open.

In the distance, directly in his path, smoke rose from the chimney of a cabin. Maybe the inhabitants knew something of Black Ears and the children.

Fully awake now, Stephen kicked the horse into a gallop and arrived at the cabin minutes later. The horse snorted, the door opened, and a man emerged with a gun. He looked back inside. "It's all right. It ain't that Indian."

Stephen left the saddle. His heart thundered in his chest. "Please, did the Indian have two children with him?"

A woman, her rounded stomach protruding from beneath her threadbare dress, came out. "He did. He said he was taking them home, but—"

"How could you believe that?" A white pall of lightheadedness covered Stephen's vision.

The man grabbed his shoulder. "Whoa there, come inside. If you're those children's father, I understand why you're about to faint. I would too, as mean as that Indian was."

The man led Stephen inside to a table. The woman gave him water. After a few swallows, he splashed the rest on his face. Revived, he faced the couple. "That Indian is a Shawnee. He took my children." He eyed the man's gun, now in a rack over the fireplace. "You have a gun. Why didn't you stop him?"

"Darn thing's broke," the man said. "I was lucky I had it behind the edge of the fireplace. That's the only way I got the drop on that Indian. The way he kept eyeballin' my wife and jabbin' a knife in the table, I thought he had a mind to torture her and kill us both."

Stephen imagined the situation. The man had no means of self-defense. A hostile Indian was going to kill them. If the man was forced to use the gun, which wouldn't work, Black Ears would've killed them for sure. "You say they were inside?"

"He wanted food," the woman said. "I fried two chickens and fed them biscuits." She placed a hand to her stomach. "Your children were sweet as can be." A pan of what smelled like cornbread sat on the table. She slid it over. "I'm sorry we couldn't stop him."

"How long ago was this?" Stephen asked, hoping he was gaining on the threesome.

"Yesterday," the man said. He shoved the cornbread closer. "Eat. You look mighty poorly."

Stephen did so, washing bites down with water after a quick blessing. Thank the good Lord he was gaining on them. A fight was coming, and he would have to decide if he would—or could—kill Black Ears or not. He couldn't see any other way. Since the Shawnee carried a knife, if he saw Stephen, he could kill the children without hesitation. What a nightmare situation, one he never expected to find himself in.

The man poured himself water and sat. "You're one of them Amish, right?"

Remembering his manners, Stephen set his hat on the table. "I am. My community is in Ohio."

The man let out a soft whistle. "You come a far piece. This here's Indiana."

Done with his meal, Stephen stood. "Bless you for the meal. Please keep my children in your prayers." He didn't say the rest: *And keep me in your prayers so I'll know what to do when the time comes.*

The woman wrapped the remaining cornbread in a rag and gave it to him. On the horse, Stephen touched the wide brim of his hat. "*Gott* bless you."

He picked the trail up easily, which ran straight west. A mile later, his eyelids rose and fell, rose and fell. He had to get more sleep tonight, or he wouldn't be any good in the coming fight.

* * *

Propped against his saddle by the creek, John chewed the tough horse meat. He had smoked a fair amount over the fire, but the carcass was too far gone to use anymore. Thank goodness he was upwind, or the smell and the feeding buzzards would've made him sick.

From the moment Stephen had ridden away, John had prayed for his friend and his family, prayed for *Gott's* will to be done, prayed for no one to be harmed, prayed that if it came to it, the members of their community would forgive him because *Gott* already had.

Holding the rifle he had bought at the urging of the store owner, he tested the trigger while securing the hammer. Hair triggers weren't common on muskets, but this trigger was definitely a hair trigger. He and Stephen had practiced a few shots, both remarking at how the gun would fire with little more than a touch to the trigger, plus how accurate they were.

He set the gun aside and worked his wrist. It was still sore, but the pain was better. With his food running low, he should start back home on foot. With *Gott's* blessing, he would arrive there in a few days.

After gathering his meager belongings and filling his canteen with water, he left a message for Stephen by using rocks to write—Gone Home. See You There.—and started back along the trail that had led him here.

With every step, he prayed, *Dear Heavenly Father, please be with my friend and his family. Let nothing but Your will be done, amen.* On and on it continued. On and on he went, one foot in front of the other. Tears filled his eyes at the prospect of losing Stephen and his children, Naomi a widow, possibly growing bitter at *Gott* for allowing this to happen. John loved *Gott* with all his heart. Despite his doubts, he believed the outcome would be the best for all concerned.

Romans 12:19-21 says, "Dearly beloved, avenge not yourselves, but rather give place unto wrath: for it is written, Vengeance is mine; I will repay, saith the Lord. Therefore if thine enemy hunger, feed him; if he thirst, give him drink: for in so doing thou shalt heap coals of fire on his head."

Although Bishop Miller had taught this verse many times, using it as justification to shun violence, no one involved in this situation—except maybe for Black Ears—wanted vengeance. Everyone else wanted to rescue Timmy and Lucy, preferably without harming anyone, and to return them home.

The seriousness of the situation made John shake his head in sorrow. Black Ears, by all accounts, was the worst a man could be: a murderer, a kidnapper, and other things too harsh to repeat around ladies. He held two children captive, to do what with, no one knew. If he even got the hint that

Stephen was near, he would likely kill the children and hide in wait to kill Stephen, with an arrow ready to fly.

To the west, dark clouds gathered on the horizon, mirroring his mood. Lightning glowed inside one of the clouds. Moments later, thunder rumbled, low and ominous.

Since vengeance was *Gott's*, perhaps He would shoot Black Ears by using Stephen as His instrument of retribution. Regardless of how it occurred, not only should it occur, it *must* occur. *Evil cannot be allowed to flourish,* John thought. *Surely Gott doesn't want that, so does he want mankind to meet the challenge of fighting evil like the Archangel Michael fought Satan?*

The question troubled him. People couldn't run around harming those they thought were evil, but they should be able to defend themselves, their loved ones, and the innocent from evil.

Lightning brightened the horizon; thunder rumbled again, this time to the point of Stephen feeling its vibration in his chest. A gust of wind blew his hat from his head. He chased it down and donned it, pressing it firmly over his sweat-soaked hair.

Water from the canteen soothed his thirst. Smoked meat eased his appetite. He continued on, plodding forward on the dusty ground, both hoping and not hoping for rain. If the storm came, it might ruin the tracks, and Stephen would lose the trail. That was worse than being hot and sweaty and needing a deluge to rinse the stink from both body and clothing.

The storm went south. A curtain of gray marked the rain pummeling the good earth. The outgoing breeze brought its smell to John. He loved that smell, loved the promise of crops growing, flowers blooming, trees budding, each a gift from almighty *Gott*.

Toward dusk, a grove of maples made a decent place for camp. Missing the saddle he left at the creek, he rested his head on a clump of moss, repeated his prayers for *Gott's* will to be done, and waited for sleep.

* * *

Kneeling by his bed, having prayed as hard as he knew how, Bishop Miller wiped tears from his eyes. For the first time in his life, because of the verses his congregation had used to explain how using violence to defend someone should be acceptable, he doubted his *Ordnung.* Was the knowledge in the Bible why some bishops stayed with traditional verses, or why they didn't always preach from it, or why they didn't always recommend reading it to their congregation? If so, what good came from an *Ordnung* that followed parts of the Bible instead of all of it?

Those verses were clear: a person could defend themselves from a thief and not be held responsible if the thief died, and Jesus did have His disciples trade their garments for swords.

Rubbing his temples, he stood. Trying to figure it out had given him a headache.

He left the bedroom. In the living area to the right of the cooking area, two of his and Anna's daughters, Sarah age three and Eliza age five, were playing with faceless dolls. Mary, age eight, sat at the kitchen table with a schoolbook. Anna, the love of his life, sat in a ladderback chair by the fireplace with her knitting. She looked over her shoulder at him but said nothing, likely understanding his heartbreak at the Ebersole's tragic situation.

He sipped water from the dipper. Usually cool and sweet, it tasted of bitterness. If a murderer like Black Ears took his family, how could he do nothing to save them? Was that truly what *Gott* intended, or did Amish leaders pick and choose the parts of the Bible they decided to follow for the *Ordnung*, shunning the rest to keep community members from making decisions on their own, even if those decisions were influenced by the Bible?

He clenched his eyes shut, hoping his headache would end. A gentle hand touched his shoulder. "I'm so sorry you must bear this burden," Anna said. "It truly is a tragedy, not only for Stephen and Naomi, but for our community. I didn't care for when the prayer meeting turned into a discussion over our *Ordnung*, but I understand why. If our girls were taken, I would be torn apart with wanting to save them."

Levi opened his eyes. "That discussion was more like an argument." He patted his wife's hand. "I agree about our girls. I doubt I could stand by and do nothing if they were taken."

Anna slipped her hand around his waist and leaned her head against his shoulder. "Are the verses they mentioned in the Bible? If so, why can't we follow them?"

The confusion in her voice troubled Levi,

and he regretted it. No one should ever feel confused about the word of *Gott*. "Yes, those verses are there. All this time I've been using verses I learned from other bishops. Then my congregation reminds me of them. I studied them like I should've done the first time. They couldn't be clearer."

A soft cry came from Mary, whose head was down over her schoolbook. Tears fell, wetting the pages. Anna went to her and took her in her arms. "There, there, sweetheart, *Gott* will keep Timmy and Lucy safe and bring them home."

"But how?" Mary wailed. She raised her head to face Levi, breaking his heart with the tears streaming down her cheeks. "How will they come home, *Daat*, if our *Ordnung* says we shouldn't help each other when something like this happens?" She let out a pitiful sob. "Would you come for us if someone took us? Please say you would. Please, *Daat*, please say you would."

Sarah and Eliza pattered over. "What's wrong with Mary?" Eliza asked.

Four pairs of concerned and confused eyes stared at Levi—eyes waiting for an answer, and the only answer he could give them came from the Bible. He sat beside Mary, took her face in his hands. "Of course I would come for you." He wrapped his arms around his beloved family. "I would come for *all* of you." As he said this, tears burned his own eyes. But would he be able to kill if it came to it?

Dear Gott, if I've made the wrong decision, please forgive me. I must care for my community the best way I know how—straight from Your word in the Bible—and if I have to take a life to do so, I'll do what I must.

Chapter 13

At home, Naomi picked at her supper. Although the vegetable pie, made from last year's canned carrots, peas, celery, and onions in a rich sauce, smelled delicious, each time she raised a spoonful to her mouth, nausea slithered from her stomach to her throat as if it were a snake slithering through a crack in the henhouse wall. Still, since she was eating for two, she forced it down.

Done with the dishes, she covered her shoulders with a shawl and went outside to watch the sunset, but was shocked by what she saw. Clouds as black as the approaching night blotted out the western horizon, and the barest hint of lightning brightened and died within them.

She hoped this wasn't a warning of her family's death, sent to her by *Gott*. She'd rather it be a warning of Black Ears' death, but she knew that was the wrong thing to hope for. The right thing to hope for was for no one to be harmed.

Inside, darkness cloaked her home. Leaving the shawl on to ward off the chill of fear, she took the family Bible to the kitchen table and sat. Then she lit the lamp and clasped her hands together to pray out loud, as earnestly as she knew how.

"'Rejoice always, pray without ceasing, give thanks in all circumstances; for this is the will of *Gott* in Christ Jesus for you.'"

"'Rejoice always, pray without ceasing, give thanks in all circumstances; for this is the will of *Gott* in Christ Jesus for you.'"

"'Rejoice always, pray without ceasing, give thanks in all circumstances; for this is the will of *Gott* in Christ Jesus for you.'"

On and on she continued into the night. Sometimes tears trickled like a creek. Sometimes they flowed like a river. Sometimes they became a raging flood. Regardless, *Gott's* words never faltered on her lips, especially the part: "' … for this is the will of *Gott* in Christ Jesus for you.'"

Yes, the important thing is *Gott's* will, not man's will. Men wrote their *Ordnung*. Unless it used all of *Gott's* word, it could very well be flawed. Without a doubt, no believer in *Gott's* word wanted to harm anyone, yet some situations, such as her family's, might call for it.

She forced her hands apart, having prayed for hours. Straightening her back, she winced at its stiffness, plus the pain in her neck from leaning over for so long. At the bason, she washed her face and unpinned her hair. Then she donned her nightgown and climbed into bed, facing the window, beyond which an endless quilt of brilliant stars illuminated the eastern sky.

Could her family see these same stars? Could they be praying the same prayers?

Naomi certainly hoped so.

She pressed a kiss to her fingertips and shared it with Stephen's pillow.

"Do *Gott's* will, my beloved husband. If you do, everything will be all right."

* * *

Standing from the bedside, Levi rubbed his knees, sore from hours of pressing against the wooden floor. In bed by a sleeping Anna, he blew the lamp out on the nightstand and closed his eyes.

He didn't need to imagine his flock praying for its members out in the world, struggling for their lives. Without a single doubt, he knew their words were rising to *Gott*, knew *Gott* was listening to their tearful pleas, knew Jesus too, at *Gott's* side, was listening as well.

"Thy will be done," Levi murmured. "Thy will be done."

167

* * *

Astride a new horse, John yawned, weary from his days of travel since meeting two men taking a herd to sale at some town he had never heard of. The men gave him a rat-eaten saddle too, glad to be rid of it, then wished John well. With the turn of events, two hours from the creek, he knew *Gott's* hand had affected his journey. Now he was on Stephen's trail, anxious to find him before he found Black Ears. One man might stop that savage, but two would have a better chance.

Regardless of his anger, evidenced by thinking of Black Ears as a savage, he had been praying all night to not be forced to harm him, continually asking for *Gott's* will to be done in the matter.

To the east, stars glittered in the sky. To the west, where John was heading, a distant storm rumbled ominously. As fast as he had been traveling, keeping the horse at a steady trot, he hoped to catch Stephen soon.

Lightning struck up ahead. Thunder followed, much louder than before. The storm was coming, and John feared it would ruin Stephen and his children's trail. He dug his heels into the horse's flanks, urging it into a gallop.

Please, Lord, let me find my friend and his children soon. I can't bear the thought of returning home without them.

* * *

Huddled beneath a scrub evergreen tree in a section of woods, soaked to his skin, Stephen gripped the horse's reins to keep it from bolting into the storm. Anger burned through his veins—anger at the storm washing the trail away, anger at Black Ears for taking his children, anger at the men who wrote his *Ordnung* without regard to life and death situations like the one Timmy and Lucy were in. No doubt those men would say it was blasphemous to have a different opinion. No doubt they believed

169

he should let his children die because they would go to Heaven. Who were mere men to force their wills on others, picking and choosing from the Bible to enforce their wills instead of *Gott's* will? Stephen supposed they had their reasons, and he wish he knew them. At the moment, those reasons made no sense.

The rain slowed to a patter. The pull on the horse's reins eased. Lightning brightened the sky, this time far away, followed by a single boom of thunder.

Stephen tilted his head to one side. Had he heard someone yelling in anger?

* * *

"I'm wet and cold," Lucy said. "Why didn't you make the fire under a tree?"

"Me too," her brother said. "You didn't hunt anything to eat before the storm came either."

Sitting cross-legged beneath the dear skins, Black Ears tried to ignore them, but

170

their whining voices grated on his nerves. "I built a good fire. It is not my fault it rained."

"It's your fault we're hungry," Timmy said.

Black Ears ground his teeth hard enough to crush stone. "The rain is stopping. If you get more wood, I'll make a fire." He was hungry himself, having run out of the smoked deer meat long ago. The boy and girl didn't move, so he waved his hand. "Go and find wood. You said you were cold."

"In the dark?" Lucy asked.

"The storm is leaving. Find it by starlight."

The children rose. Their faint black forms started leaning over to pick up dead sticks and bringing them back.

The cold stiffened Black Ears' joints. Why was he out here when he could be with his people, with plenty of food, a warm fire, and a dry home, away from whining children? He could find his people much faster without the boy and girl if he cut their throats and left them here. He fingered the handle of his knife. Let them gather plenty of wood. Then he would build a fire to last until morning, cut their throats, and sleep peacefully for the first time since he took them.

* * *

As the starlight brightened the trail through the woods, John urged the horse on. Following hoofprints filled with water, he stopped to look ahead. In the edge of the woods, beneath a stunted evergreen, a man crawled out. The darkened woods made it hard to see, but he raised what resembled a musket. "Who's out there?" he whispered.

"It's your Amish brother!" John yelled, thrilled at finding his friend.

"Be quiet," Stephen said, coming to the path. "I just heard someone yell." He turned and pointed. "Up that way."

In the distance, partially blocked by trees, a fire bloomed.

"It might be Black Ears," John said. "Let's tie the horses and get as close as we can."

Done with the horses, they crouch-walked toward the fire. Someone dropped wood beside it, and that someone wore a dark cloak like an Amish girl would wear.

"That's Lucy," Stephen whispered.

John pointed. "Look in the woods gathering sticks. That's Timmy."

A dark form kneeling by the fire stood, and Stephen raised his gun. "How far away are we?"

John placed his hand on his friend's shoulder. "Are you sure about this?"

"As sure as I've ever been."

"I'd say seventy-five yards, well within range." John raised his gun. "We'll shoot at the same time."

Fingers touched triggers. Hesitant breaths plumed in the cold air. When Timmy dropped a load of sticks by the fire, Black Ears drew a knife and reached for him.

"Thy will be done," both men said.

Twin explosions ripped through the night. Twin screams from Timmy and Lucy echoed through the woods. Running toward them through the cloud of bitter smoke left by the black powder, John told Stephen to reload, which they completed as they reached the fire, breathing hard.

Black Ears lay by the fire, his left hand clutching his right shoulder. John kicked the knife away, but Timmy grabbed it. "Shoot him again, *Daat!*" he yelled. "He was going to kill us."

"Put the knife down, Son. He can't hurt you now." Stephen gave John the gun and reached for the knife. "Give it to me."

Timmy raised it over Black Ears' chest. "No! He needs to die so he can't hurt anyone else."

Lucy neared her brother. "Like *Daat* said, he can't hurt us anymore."

Timmy raised his eyes to Stephen.

174

"You're ... you're really here?"

"I am." Stephen dropped to his knees. "Don't I get a hug?"

"You came for us," Lucy wailed, falling into his arms.

Timmy threw the knife away and joined the hug. "I knew you'd come," he said tearfully. "I just knew it."

Studying Black Ears, John wondered how both he and Stephen had missed. When they had practiced, they agreed to aim to kill, because the Shawnee might still hurt the children if he were only wounded.

He waited until the group hug ended. "Stephen, did you pull the trigger? I was waiting for you to shoot."

Firelight lit Stephen's open mouth. "What? I was waiting for you to shoot too."

"Were you aiming to kill like we agreed? We're both good shots, so I don't—"

"I don't see how we missed either."

"Were you praying?" Lucy asked. "I was."

"Me too," Timmy said.

John patted his friend's shoulder. "'Thy will be done.' That's what I said right before the guns fired."

"Me too," Stephen said. "He looked up into the starlit sky. "Thank you, *Gott*. Not only did you fire our guns, you aimed one of them so it wouldn't kill."

"Your god is weak," Black Ears groaned. "Or I wouldn't have been able to take your children."

Timmy went to him. "Move your hand so I can see your shoulder."

"For what?" Black Ears spat. "So you can put dirt in the wound?"

"He's showing you the real strength of our *gott*," Stephen said. "He's showing you his compassion."

"What is that word? I never heard it."

"Nor felt it either," John said. "You were about to kill him, but he wants to help you."

"Exactly," Lucy said, nodding. "That's

176

compassion."

Stephen knelt by Black Ears. "I'm sorry one of us shot you, but I couldn't let you take my children. Don't you love your children enough to keep someone from taking them?"

Saying nothing, Black Ears uncovered his wound.

John came over and opened the buckskin shirt. "It's not too bad." He told Black Ears to roll over. "It's a flesh wound. It went all the way through without hitting bone. It should heal, but you can't travel."

Black Ears returned to his back. "Travel where? Back to your sheriff so he can hang me?"

Stephen lay a deer skin over him. "We'll talk about that in the morning." He faced John. "You and the children get some rest. I'll keep an eye on him."

Chapter 14

After sunrise, evidenced by yellow light filtering through the trees with their new leaves growing, the soreness in Black Ears' shoulder woke him.

Across from the fire, Timmy and Lucy slept as usual, in each other's arms, except their father lay with them, his arm around them protectively. Sitting against a tree behind them, the Amish man called John, his gun across his lap, touched his hat brim. "How's your shoulder?"

During the last three days and nights, Black Ears had tried to understand these men and their ways. To help a man who was about to kill two children made no sense. "It feels hot."

The man stood. "You've heard our names over the last three days, but we haven't been formally introduced. I'm John, and the children's *daat* is Stephen." He came over and knelt, opened the buckskin shirt and frowned. "I was afraid this might happen. Some of your shirt might've gotten in the wound, and it's infected."

"It's just as well," Black Ears said. "I'm ready to die." He didn't say the rest: *So I can be with my wife and children again.*

Stephen stood; the exhausted children didn't. He brought more wood for the fire and started a pot of coffee. Then he took his gun with him into the woods for game, which he and John had been doing since they arrived. Not long after he left, a single gunshot announced breakfast, and he returned, dragging a deer.

Timmy rose and rubbed his eyes. "Aw, *Daat.* I wanted to go hunting too."

"Come over and help me skin this doe."

179

Blinking like an owl, Lucy stood as Stephen opened the doe's legs and inserted a knife under the skin. "Ewww."

Stephen grinned. "You don't complain when you're eating it."

John faced them. "His shoulder's infected."

Stephen's lips tightened. "I'd like to get home. I'm sure Naomi's worried sick."

"She was sick before we left," Lucy said.

Stephen chuckled: a man with an interesting secret, Black Ears guessed.

"What's funny about *Maam* being sick?" Timmy asked.

"You'll find out when we get home," Stephen said, patting his son's shoulder.

Lucy's eyes widened. "Oh, *Daat!* Is it what I think it is?"

Feeling the burn of tears, Black Ears looked away. His own daughter had been thrilled with the news of having a new brother or sister. How he missed his family, so similar to this one. He faced them again. "Why do you stay when you could let me die? You want to get home like I would, if I were you."

John took a piece of the deer meat from Stephen, skewered it on a stick and leaned it over the fire. "My grandfather was Shawnee. He taught me how to track, which is how Stephen and I found you. He also taught me how the Shawnee value family." He turned the deer meat. "If you think about it, despite our differences, people are more alike than we care to admit."

"I agree." Stephen skewered a piece of meat and gave it to Lucy to cook. "We Amish wear the same clothes to avoid pride, but the *Englisch* often wear clothes to *show* pride. What good is an expensive dress and jewelry, or a fine suit and hat, when the heart is poor in spirit? Things don't bring anyone happiness. Looks don't either. Things eventually turn to dust. Looks fade with time. The important thing is realizing how we're all the same whether we admit it or not. We don't set ourselves apart with our clothes because of pride. We do so to be a community with like minds and spirits, brought together by our faith in *Gott*."

John took more meat from Stephen, skewering it for Timmy and Lucy, and offered Black Ears his portion. "Eat. You need it to get well."

"No. Just let me die."

John quickly ate the portion. "I'm not going to let that happen. *Gott* spared you for a reason. I'll be right back." He left to search in the woods, eventually kneeling and digging a root. After bringing it back, he made a poultice of it and wrapped it to both sides of Black Ears' wound with a strip of cloth torn from Lucy's dress. "That's burdock root. I pray it helps."

Black Ears was tempted to remove the poultices. Instead, he asked for deer meat, and Lucy gave him hers.

"You never told us if you have children and grandchildren."

He chewed a bite, tasteless because he felt the urge to share his story. Did that mean he was weak, and these people were stronger? No, not really. They—and their god—had showed compassion for him, a known enemy, something he had never heard of amongst his tribe. He finished the deer and rolled over to face everyone, imagining them to be his people—people who used to respect him as chief. Sensing his coming words, they're eyes, filled with curiosity instead of judgement, met his.

"When I was a young man with a young wife, we had two beautiful children." He nodded toward Stephen. "Like your two children. An Iroquois war party killed my wife and took our children." Black Ears swallowed the emotion filling his throat. "I won't say what happened to them because it is too terrible to relive."

Stephen shook his head. "I'm sorry for

what happened. When John and I guessed you had taken Timmy and Lucy, my heart was filled with vengeance at first. Then I remembered *Gott's* words about His will being done. When we shot at you, we asked for that to happen. I'm glad you weren't killed."

"Which brings me to a question," John said. "You took Stephen's children like the Iroquois took yours. Did you think vengeance against anyone, let alone the Iroquois, would clean the anger from your heart?"

"How can the deaths of my family be cleaned from my heart?" Black Ears spat.

"I don't mean it that way," Stephen said. "You'll always hurt from what the Iroquois did to your family, but your need for vengeance is what's filling your heart. I imagine that's why you took my children, and they had nothing to do with what happened to your family."

"Don't you want to see them again?" Lucy asked.

"You can if you want to," Timmy added.

Black Ears didn't hesitate. "Mishe Moneto will take me to them."

"I know that name," John said. "My grandfather told me about your Great Spirit. I'm sorry to tell you this, but you'll never see your family if you rely on a *gott* that doesn't cleanse the vengeance from your heart. Only one *gott,* through Jesus, can do that. That's the only way to see your family again."

Black Ears started to scoff at such a thing. Who were these people to tell him what god to believe? But Timmy and Lucy waiting patiently for his reaction—their innocent eyes so much like his own children's eyes—made him curious about something.

"Who is Jesus?"

Stephen finished his deer meat and set the stick aside. He drank water from John's canteen and passed it around. After everyone drank, including Black Ears, he faced him. "You're a father like the Amish consider all people the children of *Gott*. You raised your children to treat your tribe with respect, and you and your wife with respect. If they disobeyed you, you punished them, but what if they continued to disobey you? You love them dearly, but they must learn from their mistakes. You understand they will make mistakes, but you hope they will see the error of their ways and return to you. Still, they need to understand a payment must be made for losing their way. That's where Jesus comes in."

"Exactly," John said. "Jesus is *Gott's* son. He came into the world to be a payment for our mistakes, which we call sins. Instead of us, *Gott's* beloved children, paying those sins, for we can never pay for the sins of all mankind, Jesus took our sins onto himself and died to make a way for us to be forgiven for our sins."

"I don't understand," Black Ears said. "Do you mean your god killed his own son because he loved everyone else more?"

"Not at all," Lucy said. "Jesus chose death because He and *Gott* love us all the same."

"That's right," Timmy chirped while nodding his head. "It's a mirkle."

Grinning, Lucy poked his arm. "It's miracle, not 'mirkle.'"

Astonished, Black Ears couldn't imagine a god who loved everyone the same. "Do you mean *Gott* loves the Iroquois too, even though they are cruel?" Before anyone could answer, he raised his hand. "Don't say anything," he said, hanging his head in shame.

"I understand," John said. "My grandfather said different tribes from the ocean in the west to the one in the east war against each other." He reached over the fire's embers and touched Black Ears' shoulder. "Mankind wars all over the world. They kidnap and enslave each other

187

like the tribes do too. The Africans sold their slaves to the Europeans, and they took them to many other countries to work, even here. I don't like it, and I'm glad the Amish don't have slaves."

Black Ears raised his head. "So people all over the world are cruel, but *Gott* loves them the same?"

"He loves them enough to sacrifice His Son for their sins. 'For *Gott* so loved the world, that he gave his only begotten Son, that whosoever believeth in him should not perish, but have everlasting life.'"

Black Ears had never heard such beautiful words. To have everlasting life meant he could be with his wife and children for all time. A violent chill shook him. He returned to his back and pulled the deer skins up to his chin.

John came over and touched his forehead. "You've got a fever. Rest and let the poultice work."

Black Ears slowly shook his head. Above him, the trees hazed in and out, in and out. He would be with his family soon, if—"What must I do to cleanse my heart?"

Stephen went to his side. Then Timmy and Lucy did too. "You have to admit you're a sinner first," Lucy said. "That you've done bad things."

"I admit it," Black Ears said, remembering every arrow he drew, every spear he threw, every life he had taken, every child he had stolen. Like a black shroud, guilt swept over him. In his chest, his heart felt like a mountain pressing against his spirit.

Timmy took him by the hand. "Now pray this—Dear *Gott*, I know I'm a sinner. I know you sent Jesus to die for my sins. Please forgive me and accept me into Heaven when I die."

As Black Ears prayed, a portal of light opened above him. Then a petite hand, brown and slender, reached down to almost touch his face. *I always told you there was more to Mishe Moneto than our shaman told us. Before I died, I prayed you would understand one day. Now you do.*

A torrent of tears flooded his eyes. *I should've listened. I want to be with you and the children so much.*

His wife's hand withdrew to just outside the portal of light. *Not yet, my love. God, or as your new friends call Him, Gott, spared you for a purpose. Can you guess what it is?*

Black Ears nodded. *I know. Thank you for loving me. Please tell the children I'll be with you all when my work is done.*

Good bye, Wise Bear. Until we meet again.

Murmuring voices brought Black Ears back to the present. Kneeling around him, John and Stephen, Timmy and Lucy, were praying, eyes closed, hands clasped.

"Dear *Gott*, Black Ears knows he's a sinner. He knows you sent Jesus to die for his sins. Please forgive him and accept him into Heaven when he dies."

Black Ears wept like he did when his family was taken, but this time he sobbed with gratitude for these fine people. He touched Stephen's hand. "Please forgive me for taking your children and causing you such heartache."

The Amish father opened his eyes. "I forgive you, Black Ears."

Sharing a soft smile, Black Ears pressed his hand to his chest. "I am Wise Bear. That was my name before evil stole my heart." He clasped his hands and closed his eyes.

"Dear *Gott*, I know I am a sinner. I know you sent Jesus to die for my sins. Please forgive me and accept me into Heaven when I die."

Like a brilliant sunrise over the horizon on a clear spring day, a flash of light burst within his eyes. Then the weight of anger and the lust for vengeance lifted from his heart, from his chest, until it left him completely. A cool breeze caressed his brow, and he knew it was the fingertips of his wife welcoming him into the community of those who believed in *Gott's* Son, Jesus.

He wept openly when once he would've ducked his head in shame, afraid to show his weakness, which he now knew to be strength.

Around him, his new friends unclasped their hands and opened their eyes. Each one smiled brightly, sure his prayers were answered.

"Look at you," John said. "I do believe you're a new man, Wise Bear."

Wise Bear gripped John's hand. "A new man indeed." He grinned, unashamed of his snaggle-toothed appearance. "A new man with work to do."

John touched his forehead. "Only after the poultice works. Let's see how you feel in the morning."

Stephen and his children returned to the other side of the fire. "What kind of work?"

Stephen asked.

"I am going to find my people and tell them what happened because I took your children. On my journey, I will make a song about it and sing it to them when I arrive. I want them to feel the same love I feel even though I don't deserve it—the love of *Gott* through His Son, Jesus."

"We haven't told you everything about Jesus," John said. "Another important thing is how he was tortured and killed. Then he rose from his tomb on the third day. We call that day Easter."

Stephen raised a hand and counted his fingers twice. "Praise *Gott*. Today is Easter, Wise Bear, and you found Jesus with an Easter Prayer."

"And we'll miss Easter supper," Timmy complained.

"I am sorry, Wise Bear said. "And I mean for everything."

Feeling a harsh chill, he pulled the deer skins up around his neck.

"You look worse," Timmy said.

John sighed. "I was hoping the leather from your shirt would work its way out of the wound. He drew a knife from the sheath on his side. "I better get it out."

Stephen cut a piece of leather from his saddle and offered it to Wise Bear. "You might need to put this between your teeth."

As John heated the knife in the fire to not infect the wound further, Wise Bear put the leather between his teeth. Stephen opened his shirt, removed the poultice, and moved aside for John, who knelt beside Wise Bear. "Are you ready?"

Wise Bear nodded, and the tip of the knife probed the wound. Although he grunted in pain, he knew it couldn't compare to the pain *Gott* felt when His own Son died for the sins of the entire world.

John's eyes narrowed. "It's deeper than I'd hoped. Just a little more."

The warm knife probed deeper, pulsing a

searing pain through Wise Bears' arm and into his fingertips. Tears rolled from his eyes and left warm tracks down the sides of his head to pool in his ears.

John raised the knife; a tiny piece of bloody leather clung to the blade. "Stephen, let's make him another fresh poultice and let him rest. He should be better in a few of days."

Wise Bear took the leather from his mouth. "You need to go home. You've been away long enough."

Having turned away to not see the bloody ordeal, Lucy and Timmy faced them. They said nothing, but they looked at each other with downturned eyes: two children who wanted to feel their mother's arms around them.

John Faced Stephen. "Do you know how to get back? The rain probably washed the trail away."

"I doubt it. What about you?"

Wise Bear chuckled. "He is part Shawnee.

He can track the trail a bird leaves in the sky."

John laughed. "I'm not *that* good, but I can find my way home. " He faced Stephen. "You better wait with me."

Wise Bear closed his eyes, weary from controlling the urge to scream during his ordeal with the knife. If these people were examples of all the Amish, what a world it could be if it were filled with their values instead of being filled with selfishness and cruelty. He had known many Shawnee leaders. Some boasted of their power and how many wives and horses they had. No doubt, leaders like that existed everywhere in the world—leaders who cared more about wealth and power than the people they vowed to serve. Black Ears was such a leader, but Wise Bear was not. With his last breath, he would share his story of being born again—as a new man—with anyone who would listen.

Chapter 15

Sitting by the fire, his appetite renewed, Wise Bear took a bite of a turkey leg. Across from him, his new friends were enjoying roasted turkey also. Timmy gnawed on the other leg. Lucy daintily picked meat from a wing. The men licked their lips. One held a thigh, the other a piece of breast meat. Their beards shined with grease. edit

Since he woke without a fever today, three days after John removed the leather from the wound, they decided to part after lunch, when Timmy shot a turkey while hunting with his father. The boy had come running, dragging the huge gobbler. "Look what I got! Look what I got!"

Lucy had crossed her arms. "Then you get to pluck it and take its guts out."

"Now, now," Stephen had said. "You must learn to do those things for when you marry. It takes compromise to make a good union in *Gott's* eyes."

Timmy finished the turkey leg and wiped his mouth with his sleeve. Then he faced Wise Bear. "Do you know where your tribe went?"

"All I know is west. I suggested they find some of our people across the Mississippi. I will look there first."

"Why didn't you go with them?" Lucy asked.

"Black Ears wanted to stay for revenge. Thank *Gott* Wise Bear took his place."

"Amen to that," Timmy said. He fingered his ears. "I like my ears right where they are."

Stephen and John stood. "Take the rest of the turkey with you," John said. "Your

198

shoulder will be too sore to draw a bow anytime soon."

Stephen offered his hand. "I'm glad *Gott's* will was done. I didn't want to kill you, but I would if I had to."

Wise Bear released the hand. "I understand, and I forgive you for your intent. I would've done the same thing to save my family."

John shook the offered hand. *"Gott* bless you. May you have a safe journey and find your people."

Wise Bears stepped around the fire and knelt before Timmy and Lucy. "I wish I had not taken you, but I am glad I did. *Gott* made me a new man because of you."

Timmy quirked his mouth into a grin. "No, sir. *Gott* made you a knew man because of Jesus."

A single tear shimmered in the corner of one of Lucy's eyes. "I'm sorry you lost your family."

"I am too," Wise Bear said. "But now I

know I will see them again one day."

The foursome climbed into their saddles. Moments later, they were heading east, along the path through the woods. Timmy and Lucy looked over their shoulders and waved.

As Wise Bear returned the waves, his astonishment at his situation grew. Here he was, a new man with a new god—*the* god— and the one thing he wanted to do most in life was to share the news of Jesus with his people.

* * *

At Sunday morning services, Naomi could hardly keep her eyes open or her tears from flowing. Stephen and John had been gone two weeks, and she had been praying almost non-stop for them to return with Timmy and Lucy, but hope was quickly fading from her heart.

A few days ago, Bishop Miller had suggested a memorial service for them, to which Naomi and Susan had gasped and accused him of having no faith. They immediately regretted their words, admitting as such, and the bishop said to not worry, because he completely understood.

Truth be known, Naomi was thinking of moving back to Pennsylvania, where her parents were from. Although she hadn't told anyone, she had begun planning it by gathering the things she would take. It felt like a betrayal to do so, but to stay here without her loved ones would only remind her of their deaths every minute of every day.

Bishop Miller ended the sermon. After everyone sang *Jesus My Shepherd*, he gazed at them from near the fireplace.

"This is a sad day, for our brethren have been gone two weeks. I think it's time to accept *Gott's* will in this matter. He has—"

On trembling legs, Naomi stood. "I know what you're going to say." A sob shook her, and she raised a handkerchief to her eyes. "I agree. It's time to say goodbye to my family."

Beside her on the pew, Susan stood and clasped Naomi's hand. "I'm afraid we must say goodbye to John too. Her hand flew to her mouth; heaving sobs followed.

In the pews, ladies wiped tears, and men blinked to keep from doing so, many failing.

In Bishop Miller's throat, the muscles tightened with a hard swallow: a man trying to avoid sobs himself. "I understand how we all feel. I've asked myself what I would do if my family were taken, as I'm sure many others here have, and the only conclusion is that I must. Some who haven't suffered this ordeal might ask, 'Oh, but aren't you acting with free will?' My answer would be to define *Gott's* will, for if we are able to exercise free will, how do we not know it is not His will when we do so?"

Several heads nodded, with a few

"Amens" scattered about.

Naomi and Susan sat. No doubt, Naomi knew, her best friend was as comforted by the bishop's words and their congregation's compassion as she was.

"Saying that," he continued, "I suppose we should plan for a memorial service."

A man stood. "How do we have a service without—" He faced Naomi. "Forgive me, but I only want to know how we have a service without bodies."

More sobs erupted from the congregation. One weeping couple actually left because they were crying so much.

Bishop Miller raised a handkerchief to his eyes, then lowered it. "Maybe it's too soon to discuss such things. Do you agree, Naomi and Susan?"

The door slammed open. The couple's mouths worked, but nothing came out. The man shook his head. "It's a miracle! They're all coming down the road on horseback!"

A collective gasp erupted from the entire

congregation. Both thrilled and doubtful, Naomi worked her way past pairs of knees and bolted out the door. Up the road, Stephen and John on two horses, Timmy and Lucy sharing one, all waved.

Weeping tears of joy, Naomi lifted her dress to keep from tripping on it and ran toward her loved ones. Never in her entire life had her heart been so filled with gratitude. *Thank you, Gott! Thank you, Jesus! Thy will has been done!*

Stephen slid off the horse and caught her in his arms. Regardless of the Amish customs against displays of public affection, he covered her face with kisses. "Oh, my sweetheart. I've missed you more than I can say."

Naomi returned his kisses, ending with one to his lips.

Beside them, John and Susan were kissing also.

Behind them, in a display of flapping

black dresses and bobbing white *kapps,* running black pants legs and hatless heads, the congregation hurried toward them, gathering in a circle when they neared.

After shouts of "Praise *Gott!* Praise Jesus! and "Amen!" a laughing Bishop Miller tousled his own hair. "Well, aren't we a sight? But it's well deserved."

Timmy and Lucy ran toward Naomi. She knelt to gather them into her waiting arms and covered their cheeks, kissed golden by the sun, with her own kisses. When they finally parted, she held them at arm's length. "I should either hug you to death to punish you or spank your bottoms. What were you thinking, leaving the house like that?"

Timmy poked Lucy's arm. "It's her fault. She wanted to look pretty for the boys."

At the outer edges of the circle of people, the younger members of the congregation—boys and girls from six to sixteen—grinned at each other.

Lucy stuck her tongue out at Timmy. "Phooey on you. I told you my dress had a hole in it."

"Uh-huh. From your stinky underarms."

"I remember this," Stephen said. "You two were fussing at each other about stinky underarms on the day you went missing. I say to let that subject alone."

Bishop Miller joined the reunited members of his congregation. "I'd love to hear how you all made it back well and unharmed, but I'm sure you'd like to get home. What if we have a special meal in your honor next Sunday after we meet, when you've had time to rest from your ordeal?"

"A wonderful idea," Naomi said.

Spontaneously, all the members started singing *Jesus My Shepherd*, and everyone walked back to the bishop's home for their hats and bonnets.

At the wagon, Naomi hugged Susan.

206

"Thank you so much for allowing me into your home. You are such a blessing."

Susan released her. "Thank you too. I'm sure we eased each other's days and nights for the last two weeks." Her mouth fell open. "Oh, no! I left John Jr. on the pew!" She hurried inside and returned with the baby, her bonnet covering her *kapp*. She offered Naomi her own bonnet. "I saved you a walk."

Naomi donned the black bonnet. "Thank you. Let me take you and John Jr. home so I can get my brood of missing hens home for a bath before my nose wrinkles off my face."

Stephen raised his elbow and sniffed his underarms. "Hmm. You've got a point."

During the ride home, with the horses tied to the wagon and Naomi's loved ones and neighbors in the back, she praised *Gott* over and over for his blessings. She wondered about their ordeal, though, but was afraid to ask. Stephen and the children, however, seemed in good spirits, so maybe it wasn't as bad as it could've been.

At John and Susan's cabin, they said they looked forward to the gathering next Sunday and went inside. John added he would tell Susan everything so there would be no surprises.

When Naomi stopped Rufus at home, Stephen hopped from the wagon. "I'll start drawing water for our baths. Timmy, unhitch Rufus and put him and the horses in the corral."

Naomi waved to Lucy. "Come along, young lady. We've got to heat a lot of water."

As they did, Naomi continued to thank *Gott* for His will being done. Although her curiosity about how her family and John survived their ordeal gnawed at her, especially if Black Ears had been killed, she was content to wait until Stephen told her.

But what if he and John hadn't killed him? They weren't acting like two men who regretted anything. In fact, they were as happy as she'd ever seen them. Could *Gott's* will have included Black Ears coming to know Jesus? If so, what a blessing that would be. Then he would want to share the news with his people—perhaps more than his people.

Yes, what a blessing that would be.

Chapter 16

At the window of the log cabin, washing breakfast dishes in the basin while Lucy dried them beside her, Naomi watched Stephen showing Timmy and Joan how to clean Rufus's hoofs. She had hoped Joan would be a boy so she could name him John, in honor of how their loyal friend had helped Stephen reunite her family three years ago.

She often wondered if Wise Bear had found his people, wondered if any had come to know Jesus, wondered if he were even alive. As old as Stephen had described him when he told the story at the supper the week after they returned from their ordeal, she doubted it.

She also wondered if the once brutal savage had actually come to know *Gott*. It shamed her to do so, especially since she knew Stephen and John's words could be trusted on the matter. Still, when she imagined how many people had suffered at his hands, the doubt crept in. What it would take to force it away forever, she didn't know. At least he was gone and would never return.

Reaching for another of Rufus's hooves, Stephen looked to the north. His expression betrayed nothing. It usually did, though, with a smile when one of their community members stopped by for a visit. He pointed to the door. Timmy took Joan by the hand and hurried her inside. "*Maam*, there's an Indian coming," he said, closing the door.

Lucy ran to another window to look out. "I wonder if it's Wise Bear?"

Naomi eyed the musket hanging over the fireplace. Stephen would've come for it if he thought there was trouble. She told the children to stay inside and joined him.

Astride a brown horse with white

splotches on its rear, the man wore boots, pants with suspenders, a buckskin shirt, and a wide-brimmed leather hat, like some of the people called cowboys wore. The only sign he was an Indian was his black hair down his back. He also had a musket in a scabbard tied to the saddle.

As he neared, he raised his hand in welcome and dismounted the horse. "Good morning. Are you the Ebersole family?"

"We are," Stephen said. "I'm Stephen and my wife is Naomi. How can we help you?"

"My name is Little Cub. I'm a friend of Wise Bear. I've come a long way to see you."

"Have you eaten breakfast?" Naomi asked. "I have some leftovers if you'd like."

Little Cub offered a smile. "Thank you, no. I ate in town." He glanced at the cabin. "Wise Bear told me about your children. Are they inside? Some of what I have to tell you is not for children's ears."

"Would you like some coffee?" Stephen

asked. "We can talk in the barn while Naomi makes sure the children stay inside."

"Lucy can do that," Naomi said, knowing she must hear what Little Cub was going to say about Wise Bear. Inside, she filled three cups, told the children to stay put, and joined Stephen and Little Cub in the barn, where they were sitting in the rear of the wagon.

Little Cub took the offered cup and sipped. "Very good, thank you." He set the cup beside him and removed his hat. "I've come to tell you … Wise Bear died six months ago."

"That's a shame," Stephen said. "I hope he passed peacefully."

A single twitch in Little Cub's cheek said otherwise. "I'm Shawnee. Wise Bear found us a few months after he left you. He told everyone your story. I was the only one who believed him. We decided to leave and tell as many people as we could." Little Bear drank coffee. "He learned to read when he fought with the Virginians against the red-coat soldiers. We went to the nearest town and asked the preacher if we could have two Bibles. He looked at us as if we had lost our minds, but he did give us one Bible."

"I'm sorry about that," Stephen said. "It seems that preacher needs to learn to care for everyone, not just those he thinks are Christians."

Sipping coffee, Little Cub lowered the cup. "That's what Wise Bear said. In all our travels, no one would listen. Some laughed. Some mocked. Some threatened. After they did those things, they made us leave."

The news both relieved and disappointed Naomi. Although Little Cub had confirmed Stephen and John's story about Wise Bear finding *Gott*, he had only been able to help one person do the same thing.

Little Cub blinked, looked away, and faced them again. "The last place we stopped was to speak with a tribe of

214

Iroquois. Considering Wise Bear's past with them, I questioned him about it. He said God loved them like he loved everyone, so they should hear His word. As soon as they saw us, they dragged us off our horses and tied us to a post. After a few minutes of talk, they said they would kill us the next night. They beat us before they went to sleep. I pulled the knot loose in the ropes around my wrists with my teeth. When I started to untie Wise Bear, he said to leave him, because one death might stop them from coming after me."

Naomi swallowed at the pain in the man's voice and the tears filling his eyes.

"We often spoke about the evil in the world," he continued. "He told me what you and John said about people everywhere fighting and enslaving each other. I was born a warrior, but I never had the heart for such things." He sipped coffee. "I begged him to go but he refused. He told me to take his horse because one of his saddlebags had the Bible in it. I shook his hand and left. That night, I left the horse in the woods and crawled near the village. They tied Wise Bear to a post and burned him alive. I didn't want to watch, but I thought I owed him my gratitude for how he taught me about Jesus. Before the flames consumed him, he raised his head to the stars. I think he saw his wife and children because he was smiling."

Stephen fingered tears from his eyes. "You were blessed to have known him, Little Cub. His story proves how people can change if they repent. I pray more do. The world seems to be filling with more and more evil every day."

Little Cub stood from the wagon. "Thank you for the coffee. I thought you'd like to know the end of Wise Bear's story. Now I plan to continue it. I pray I'll meet more people who will listen than he did."

"It starts with one voice," Stephen said as he and Naomi walked with Little Cub to his horse.

"I agree," she said. "Like with Jesus's voice continuing from the time he died until now, and on and on and on."

On the horse, Little Cub touched the brim of his hat. "God bless you."

As he rode away, the children came outside. Little Cub looked over his shoulder and smiled and waved, and everyone returned both.

"Who was he?" Timmy asked.

"A friend of Wise Bear," Stephen said. "He passed on a few months ago, and he came to tell us."

"Why couldn't we listen?" Lucy asked.

Eyeing his daughter, Stephen heaved a sigh. "Your *maam* and I will tell you after Joan's in bed."

"Oh," Timmy said: a boy who knew his *daat's* tone meant it wasn't a peaceful death.

After the quiet trio returned to the cabin, Naomi faced Stephen. "You know I trust you and John, but I've been questioning your story about Wise Bear ever since you told it. I'm sorry. I shouldn't have done that. He represented the worst of men, but even he changed to represent the best of men."

Stephen's chest rose and fell with a heavy breath. "I pray more people will change like he did. Like the people in town, too many are only concerned about one thing—themselves."

Wanting to end the talk on a lighter note, Naomi placed her husband's hand on her tummy. "Well, this is another member of this family who we'll make sure to teach to care about others."

Stephen grinned. "Oh, I know about that. I heard you vomiting this morning."

Naomi poked his stomach. "And you didn't even get out of bed to hold my hair for me. What kind of husband *are* you?"

Stephen kissed her. "One who loves his family more than he can say, like Wise Bear loved his."

He looked up into the brilliant blue sky. "Rest in peace, my friend. Rest in peace."

Dear reader,

Thank you for choosing this book. If you enjoyed reading it as much as I enjoyed writing it, you *really* enjoyed it. Saying that, please enjoy the first chapter of *Clara's Mourning*. It's the first book in what I call my Clara Engelman Series, available now at Amazon. The second book, *Clara's Courtship*, will be published on May first. The third book, *Clara's Choice*, will be published June first.

Torn between admiration for the sunrise and the need to keep her memories of Abram tucked away like a chaste kiss, Clara didn't know whether to smile or cry. She had enjoyed similar scenes with him after they were married, but the one before her, nor the ones to come, would never compare. Still, the beauty of the breaking day was a gift from God, and it was worthy of her attention.

The shimmering line of crimson above

the horizon lit the distant treetops with flame. The first air of dawn stirred, cold and brisk. In the chicken coop behind the barn, the rooster crowed. In the maple tree beside the single-story home clothed with white-painted boards, two bluebirds left their house attached to the trunk and fluttered to a limb to warble their waking song.

Clara's footsteps crunched in the greening grass. Her breath plumed before her face and dissipated as it shrouded her cheeks with white. She entered the dark kitchen and left the basket of eggs and the still illuminated flashlight on the table to light her way. For a moment she considered checking on Edna and John but didn't. Her footsteps, no matter how soft, might wake them if she approached their room, and they needed all the sleep they could get.

She paused for water. At the sink, sipping from the glass, she leaned closer to the window. Over the hill between her farm and the neighbor's farm, the rising sun etched the first rays of yellow into the sky. It was the first of April in southern Virginia, still capable of frost, and she had forgotten her mittens while gathering eggs, leaving her hands chilly from the morning cold.

She finished the water and went to the cookstove to add wood to the glowing embers. Leaving the cast iron door open, she pulled a chair over from the table and sat to warm her hands near the opening.

How she missed Abram's warm embraces in the nights, now long and lonely after his funeral a month ago. His death had left a hole in her life like a well without water: cold and damp, without the least bit of comfort. Four-year-old Edna and three-year-old John missed their papa as well, evidenced by the nightmares that still woke them at least three times a week. Thankfully, they had slept the last two nights without crying, nor asking when he would return from that terrible dark hole in the earth, now filled beneath the old oak tree behind the house.

Although she and Abram had been teaching them about their Heavenly home, they were too young to understand, much less understand about death. Regardless, Clara had tried to explain how living things died, using the example of a hen that had died of old age a few days after the funeral. All the children had managed was to look at her with huge, questioning eyes rimmed with tears.

The rooster crowed again, followed by more of the bluebird's warbling entering the screened door. She had left the wooden door open to remind her to milk the cow, one of the many chores that were now left to her alone.

Tears threatened. She attempted to blink them away.

Not only was she forced to endure life without Abram's love, she was forced to try to keep the farm profitable enough to feed her family and pay the bills.

Clara palmed the wetness from her eyes. How could she do all that without help? Not only had she never hitched the plow to their used tractor, she didn't know how to drive it, much less how to maintain it. At least she had two seasons of vegetables canned, so she and the children had plenty to eat, and the chickens would provide eggs and meat.

She bowed her head for a prayer of thanks for her Beachy Amish Mennonite brothers and sisters, who had built the coffin and helped with the funeral, and with bringing enough food so cooking hadn't been necessary for a week. She also appreciated their vows to continue helping, including with money, but it felt wrong to Clara to not earn her own way.

Even Bishop Silverman had calmed the children by saying all would be well, that their papa would never stop loving them and watching over them. If only Clara could've been comforted by those words.

Looking for a new area with large acreage for sale, plus being frugal with their meager funds, she and Abram had bought this farm. Tucked away in a somewhat isolated area in Charlotte County, it was a late wedding gift to each other with the money his and her parents had given him. Unfortunately, her and Abram's parents lived in Pennsylvania, where their other children lived. Yes, they had made the drive for the funeral, but they had returned shortly after, saying they were needed back home.

Noting how the wood wasn't catching fire in the embers, Clara adjusted it with a poker until it flamed.

The smell of woodsmoke brought back the memory of her and Abram's first night here together, snug in several quilts in front of this very wood stove, the door open on a freezing January evening. Although they slept that way when it was bitterly cold, it was an adventure too, enjoyed in the early days of their marriage.

Rising from the chair, she shut the door and rose to get the pail for the milk. She considered the mittens on the shelf above the coat rack, but she wouldn't be able to roll her fingers properly as she milked, and the cow sometimes kicked if she felt something different.

Clara paused for another swallow of water. In the window over the sink, her reflection stared back. She'd risen and put on Abram's pants and wide-brimmed hat, both warmer than her dress and the bandana she tied over her hair while she worked. She'd also put on two pair of his socks and his work boots, leaving her looking nothing like the proper Beachy Amish housewife. Then again, the farm was over twenty miles away from the community she belonged to, a newer one north of the Amish community in Nathalie, Virginia, in Halifax County, so she wouldn't be caught out of her traditional clothing. Even if she were, she had arrived at the point of not caring, which she *didn't* care for.

Then again, she knew God loved her regardless, and His acceptance was more important than what others thought. Also, maybe she wore Abram's clothes to recall his warmth surrounding her, like a second skin of love she would never shed.

The two bluebirds continued to warble, and the sound saddened her. She and Abram used to call their nightly talks in bed talking like the bluebirds, when they spoke of the children and their dreams for them.

Clara refused to judge other religious beliefs, but she was grateful for her and Abram's Beachy Amish Mennonite Ordnung. Still, although a used pickup truck sat by the barn, she didn't know how to drive it. They had also discussed getting a telephone when they could afford it, which they couldn't yet. They hadn't minded living simply until they could do better, but how some of the stricter Amish lived without conveniences such as indoor plumbing, Clara didn't know. She, however, admired their strength in doing so.

Peering at her reflection again, she tucked several strands of her red hair, having escaped their pins, beneath Abram's hat. She then drank another swallow of water and took the flashlight and pail to the barn to milk the cow.

Inside the two-story structure, where the aroma of hay and manure permeated the crisp air, she sat on a stool beside the cow and rubbed her hands together to warm them. Few things angered Clara like having the cow kick the pail over from cold hands.

With her palms warm, she began milking. As the metallic rhythm of the twin streams struck the side of the pale, Clara grew drowsy. She once loved the misty feeling of sitting in the quiet of the barn and listening to Abram milking the cow. Although their Ordnung allowed many modern conveniences, they preferred growing their own food and having fresh milk for butter and cheese, which they sold from a stand near the mailbox when they had extra, along with vegetables from the garden. They had bought the house from an Amish family who belonged to a stricter Ordnung. Abram had planned to have the entire home wired when he hired a man to install the electric pump for the indoor plumbing. Instead, the money was needed to repair their old pickup truck, to repair the barn's roof, and to build a pig pen and a place for them to shelter when it rained and snowed. Unfortunately, Abram had fallen from the loft and broken his neck. Yes, they had spent the money on everything except the pigs, and Clara was glad. She didn't think she could kill and butcher one without Abram's help.

The cow mooed, jarring her from her thoughts. Outside, gravel crunched in the driveway. She knew only one person in this area, so it might be the neighbor arriving in his pickup truck. Standing, Clara girded herself for a confrontation.

Jonah Ellis was one of those men who refused to believe women were equal to men. Two weeks ago, when she, Edna, and John had stopped to rest on their walk from the local market about five miles away, Mr. Ellis had come along and stopped to insist he give them a ride home. Yes, his idea was practical, but the way he looked down at her from what was likely his six-foot plus height—she being a petite five-foot four inches and as slender as a newborn whitetail fawn—had angered her. It also hadn't helped the matter any that he wasn't Amish or Mennonite, or that his honey-brown eyes seemed to pluck her nerves, or that his wavy brown hair like Abram's had caught her eye, or that he lived with the woman he was engaged to. To Clara, living together out of wedlock was like the English saying: "Why buy the cow when you can get the milk for free?"

The vehicle door slammed. Footsteps crunched toward the house. Knuckles knocked on screened door. "Mrs. Engelman? It's Bishop Silverman."

Panic struck a harsh chord inside Clara's chest. Despite not caring what others thought of her wearing Abram's clothes, she didn't know what the bishop might say. More strands of her red hair hung from beneath Abram's hat. She tucked them in, made sure the zipper of his huge canvas coat was up, and left the barn.

As Abram's heavy boots clomped in the gravel, the bishop, about to knock on the door again, turned. "Clara?"

Not only did his look of disapproval slow Clara's stride, him calling her by her first name for the first time did as well. "I was milking the cow, Bishop Silverman." She wrapped her arms around herself. "It's very cold. That's why I'm wearing Abram's things."

A single twitch in the bishop's cheek showed his further disapproval. "I … well, I suppose you need to be warm."

Clara moved closer. Her breath, hard and fast, jetted from her nostrils in twin streams, the same as from the bishop's. "I would offer coffee," she said. "The children are still asleep and I hate to wake them."

"I understand. How are you— I mean, how are they doing?" His eyes darted to one side.

Unless Clara missed her guess, the bishop was here for an unwelcome reason—one that her best friend, Alison Henley, had suggested he might attempt. Before Clara and Abram moved here, so Alison had said, the bishop's wife ran off with a man from town and filed for divorce a year later. Clara had never heard of a Mennonite man or woman divorcing. Regardless, she wasn't ready to marry again—if ever—and certainly not to Bishop Silverman.

The bishop cleared his throat. His face was red, either from the cold or embarrassment. He came closer. His hand raised to Clara's temple, where a single fingertip touched her skin. "I don't know how, but I never realized you have red hair." He licked his lips. "I came to ask—"

Clara backed away. "As you can see, I'm very busy."

"Do you need help with anything?"

"No, please. Why did you come?"

"I … well …"

Clara could see his intention in the way his eyes focused on hers. With Abram gone, the bishop had come to hover over her like a hawk seeking a mouse in the field of her mourning.

He raised his hand to her temple again. She wanted to run, to scream, to grab the pitchfork from the barn and make him leave. Instead, she simply stood there. If not, if he went back home and spread the word that he had caught her out of her dress and kapp, who knew what would happen.

The bishop withdrew his hand without touching her. "You have straw in your hair. I was only going to take it out."

Clara brushed at her hair; a piece of straw fell at her feet.

The bishop went to his pickup and returned with a huge pot covered with a lid. "This is cabbage soup I made last night. I enjoy cooking but I made too much, likely because I was thinking of my … Well, Sarah's gone, but I can't stop thinking about her. I'm sure you feel the same way about Abram."

Shame heated Clara's cheeks. This poor man missed his wife as much as she missed Abram, and he was only trying to help in any way he could. She took the pot. "Thank you for thinking of the children and me."

"You're welcome." He shoved his hands into his pants pockets. "You're right, it's very cold this morning."

Clara gave him the pot. "Please take that to the kitchen table while I get the milk I left in the barn. I'll make coffee to warm us up."

He took the pot. "I've been thinking about your situation here. You can't drive, and you live far away from our community." He paused. "You have a good neighbor in Jonah. I know him well and trust him. I'm sure he's willing to help around the farm if you need him."

Clara nodded. She could use help now and then, and it was kind of the bishop to make allowances for her situation, even for her English neighbor. Maybe she had misjudged Mr. Ellis when he had offered to give her and the children a ride. She went to the barn for the milk. In the kitchen, beside the table, the bishop faced her. "You said Edna and John are still asleep?"

Filling the percolator with water, Clara looked over her shoulder. "They still have nightmares about the funeral. Anytime they go near a hole outside, no matter how small, they run from it. I tried to explain death to them, and how they'll see their papa again, but they're too young to understand."

"Would you like me to try?" the bishop asked.

Clara noted the sincerity in his voice. "I'd rather not until they're older. They're starting to sleep better now." She finished filling the percolator, measured coffee, and took it to the stove.

Along with noting the bishop's sincere voice, she also noted the hint of gray hair at his temples, plus how he hadn't removed his wide-brimmed hat, black as a crow's breast feathers. She took Abram's coat and hat to the hanger, placed her kapp over her pinned hair, and returned to the stove, rubbing her cold hands together over the hot metal.

The bishop took her cue and hung his coat and hat on the peg beside hers, which caused a twinge of anger in her. It was as if he had taken Abram's place without asking, and she didn't like it at all. Despite her warming hands, she continued rubbing them together. Although the bishop seemed nice, she had the feeling he was watching her, possibly thinking of her as his future wife. Fear prickled along the back of her neck.

"Mrs. Engelman?"

Clara refused to turn. At least he had called her by her married name. "Yes?"

"If I'm making you uncomfortable by being here, I can leave."

His voice was soft and gentle. Shame heated Clara's cheeks again. Perhaps she was oversensitive because of losing Abram. She turned to face the patient man. "I admit it's strange having another man here with Abram gone." She paused to give her confused mind time to find the right words. "I realize you're my bishop, but …" Her hands began to tremble. She raised them to her face and spun away to cry.

If her feelings about the bishop wanting her for a wife were true, she expected him to approach her, to touch her, perhaps to place a hand on her shoulder, but none of that happened.

Behind her, his footsteps shuffled on the hardwood floor. His clothing rustled as he donned his coat. More footsteps followed. The screened door softly closed, and the gravel crunched beneath the tires as he drove away.

Clara sank to her knees. Sobs continued to wrack her body until she had to force herself to stop or risk having a sore throat. Also, she needed to wake Edna and John soon, and she didn't want a raspy voice and reddened eyes to betray her tears.

She stood to the sound of percolating coffee. The aroma rose in the steam coming from the spout, reminding her of Abram again. He loved breakfast, particularly coffee. A pang of sorrow hit again, and Clara's sobs returned.

As much as she loved her sweet and gentle husband, how long would it take until she could treasure her memories of him with joy instead heartache?

J. Willis Sanders lives in southern Virginia, with his wife and several stringed instruments.

With fifteen novels published and more on the way, he enjoys crafting intriguing characters with equally intriguing conflicts to overcome. He also loves the natural world, and, more often than not, his stories include those settings. Most also utilize intense love relationships and layered themes.

His first idea for a novel is a ghostly World War II era historical that takes place mostly in the midwestern United States, which utilizes some little-known facts about German POW camps there at the time. It's the first of a three-book series, in which characters from the first book continue their lives.

Although he loves history, he has written several contemporary novels as well, and some include interesting paranormal twists, both with and without religious themes.

He also loves the Outer Banks of North Carolina, and he has written three novels within different time frames based on the area, what he calls his Outer Banks of North Carolina Series. (Yes, they've been published, and he has more story ideas about the area.)

Also, he enjoys learning about the variations of Amish culture, which inspired his Eliza Gray and Clara Engelman series, along with *The Easter Prayer: An Amish Easter Story* and *The Forgiveness Quilt: An Amish Christmas Carol.*

Other hobbies include reading (of course), vegetable gardening, playing music with friends, and songwriting, some of which are in a few of his novels.

To follow his work, visit any of these websites:

https://jwillissanders.wixsite.com/writer

https://www.facebook.com/J-Willis-Sanders-874367072622901

https://www.amazon.com/J-Willis-Sanders/e/B092RZG6MC?ref_=dbs_p_ebk_r00_abau_000000

Readers: to help those considering a purchase, please leave a review on Amazon.com, Goodreads.com, or wherever you bought this book.
They help authors more than you may realize.

Thank you.